VICTORIAN SURPRISE

by

Lena Lane

Copyright © 2018 Lena Lane

All rights reserved. No part of this publication may be reproduced, distributed, or transmitted in any form or by any means, including photocopying, recording, or other electronic or mechanical methods, without the prior written permission of the publisher, except in the case of brief quotations embodied in the critical reviews and certain other noncommercial uses permitted by copyright law.

This book is a work of fiction. The names, characters, places, and incidents are products of the writer's imagination. Any resemblance to actual persons, places, events, business establishments or locales is entirely coincidental.

VICTORIAN SURPRISE

Lena Lane Logo Design by Gin's Book Designs (http://ginsbookdesigns.com/)

Victorian Surprise
Book Three of the Sampson Series

It's time for Sharon's story. As the baby of the Sampson family, she's got sass and plenty to say, especially to her siblings. But when she meets Jon, she's at a loss for words. Considering how many unique individuals she'd met in her real estate business, his bold and quirky ways leave her unsettled. Can she see beyond his odd behavior to the person he really is?

As a former detective, Jon has an aptitude to dig for the truth, to expose the secrets people have. And Sharon is now his target. Charming her into sharing her story with him, he knows more about her than she ever intended. Exactly how he likes it. But will he be able to reveal his own history?

Can love break the walks they've both put around their hearts?

Dedication

As always, to my family, by blood and by choice. Thank you for supporting me and for helping me do this.

To my editors and beta readers. Thank you for being my living thesaurus and for catching my inconsistencies. You make my work so much better.

But mostly to You, the reader. I hope you have as much fun reading this as I had writing it.

I love you all.

Lena

Table of Contents

Red Heels 1
The Airport 3
Strange Flight 8
Twenty Questions 13
Blue Black 19
Unspoken Dreams 24
Hesitant Departure 30
Overprotective Brothers 33
Unexpected Texts 35
Hi Honey 39
A Kiss 42
Screw Wise 48
No Talking 53
The Morning 58
A Wedding? 64
Al's Girlfriend 68
Lunch Drama 73
The Spy 78
Plus One 81
Horrible Movie 85
Cheat Day 91
Lethal Dancer 93
Vegas Night 98
Getting Ready 100
Elegant Venue 106
Al's Phone 109
Land Boats 116
Sam's Neighbors 125
Just Heels 129
Turbulent Flight 133

Nice Distraction	*138*
Separate Ways	*140*
Old Habits	*142*
Grumpy Call	*146*
Be Safe	*151*
Stalking Behavior	*158*
She's Gone	*162*
Another Agent	*165*
Swaying World	*167*
So Sorry	*168*
Mama Mabel	*173*
It's Over	*176*
Choke Hold	*178*
Merry Christmas	*182*
Old Victorian	*186*
Scheduled Showing	*189*
Bloody Concrete	*194*
Impotent Rage	*198*
Moving On	*201*
Story Time	*203*
Too Perfect	*209*
Night Sky	*212*
Closing Time	*216*
Group Effort	*219*
Such Wickedness	*223*
The Talk	*226*
Welcome Home	*229*

Red Heels

The blonde was pacing again. For the fourth time in half an hour, she had stood up from her seat and went to look at the plane. She strode purposefully to the window as if there was something important she had to do and was pressed for time. But when she got there, she simply stared at the plane for half a minute, spun around and returned to her seat.

Jonathan Rossi had to wonder why that was. He didn't need detective training to notice that she was anxious. What worried him was: Why? He hated to think that someone so beautiful could have terrorist intentions. Still, he wasn't going to let a pretty face blind him to a hideous soul. And damn, she was pretty. Using the excuse that it was his sworn duty to protect innocent lives, he gave himself permission to watch her—to determine the true cause of her pacing, of course. The fact that she was perfection in motion was irrelevant.

She looked like a porcelain doll brought to life; so pale, she looked fragile. The pin straight platinum hair that reached just below her shoulders looked like silk strands, and he wanted to run his fingers through it, just to find out if it was as silky as it looked.

Too far to know for sure, he suspected her eyes were a pale blue. But what caught his attention more than anything else were her full lips. Full, very *kissable* lips. They were a deep, ruby shade that matched her heels and nail polish. Was that done on purpose? Did she change nail polish every time she wanted to wear different color shoes?

Considering her full suit, which included a blazer, slacks, and the high heels, Jon inferred a business trip, which could result in trepidation and would, no doubt, lead to pacing. But people didn't usually bring family on business trips and Jon was fairly certain that the other two couples with her were family. The two males had similar enough features to make him believe they were siblings. Not that the blonde spent any time speaking with them. They were so engrossed in their partners that they ignored her. And she, in turn, ignored them.

If he wanted to know for sure, he was going to have to speak with her. *Oh, the things I have to do to keep others safe,* he chuckled to himself. *Speaking to a gorgeous female—such a terrible duty.* But for the sake of all the innocent people on the plane, he would make sure she was just nervous about the flight and didn't have any other ulterior, dark and dangerous, motives.

The Airport

The afternoon sky was dark, the clouds heavy with the threat of thunder and lightning. Sharon Sampson was not thrilled with the weather. She wasn't a fan of flying to begin with, and the thought of the plane cutting through those clouds—and the turbulence they'd cause—was enough to make her heart pound. Did her brothers know how much she loved them? Only for them would she force herself to do this. With a heavy sigh, she brushed her blonde hair from her face, tucking the strands behind her ear.

Sharon and said family were sitting at an airport terminal, waiting for their turn to board their plane. Impatiently, she tapped the soles of her ruby-red high heels on the tile; left, right, left, right, left, right; the sounds soothing somehow.

Seated to Sharon's right was her brother, Sam, the reason for the last minute trip, and his fiancée, Sam. Sharon had to shake her head at the ironies of life. Sam had to fall in love with a woman who also called herself Sam. Though Sharon couldn't blame him; Samantha Waters was a bright, funny, endearing woman who knew what she wanted and had the tenacity to make it happen, no matter the obstacles. And what she wanted now was a quick, "I do," in Vegas.

The eldest brother, Scott, was sitting to her left with his new bride, Sarah. Unlike Sam, Sarah was a bit more traditional and had loved her conventional wedding, including a beautiful church service and a full reception just a couple of days ago. Now, they were on their way to Fiji for their honeymoon, stopping in Vegas just long enough for Sam's wedding. After that, they were headed for sunny beaches and warm waves.

With all the love in the air, Sharon had never felt more miserable. She loved her brothers dearly, and they had fallen in love with wonderful women whom she adored. But the lovey-dovey exploits around her were going to make her vomit. Enough was enough. There was no need for the blatant PDA going on around her. To her left, the newlyweds were holding hands and speaking softly, their heads close together while they whispered about whatever they had to whisper about, sneaking occasional kisses. To her right, Samantha was chatting nonstop about what they should do in Vegas while Sammy just watched her, his arm resting on the back of her chair. Sharon's stomach turned at the pure adoration in his eyes as he gazed at his fiancée and simply listened. It was nauseating.

And stuck between the two sets of lovebirds was Sharon. By herself.

How had this happened? How was it that her brothers' counterparts were both younger than she was and yet had somehow managed to find the happily-ever-after everyone wanted? Though Sharon was happy for them, being stuck in the middle like some weird, solitary pigeon, was not her idea of a good time. After all the dates she'd been on, why hadn't she found her mate? Was it too much to ask for her version of The One?

A little voice grumbled in her head, *Where those really* dates *or were they business dinners? Because there was an awful lot of real estate talk at those* dates. *When was the last time you had dinner with someone who wasn't also your client?* She groaned softly.

VICTORIAN SURPRISE

Enough of that, she told herself firmly. There was no need to continue with the depressing thoughts.

Sharon had many strengths, but patience was not one of them. With an exasperated sigh, she stood and walked to the floor-to-ceiling windows to look at the plane they were waiting for. Again. Like her, it had nothing to do but wait. For what, though, Sharon didn't know.

She took another deep breath. There was a reason she did most things herself—because it was faster than waiting for someone else to do it, whatever *it* was. Unfortunately, she hadn't learned how to fly a plane—yet. After today, however, she might add it to her list of things to do.

Oblivious of her environment, her gaze was focused on the plane, until a deep voice startled her.

"You don't have to worry 'bout the storm." The hint of a foreign accent gave the words a sexy twist.

She turned quickly to face him, the soles of her heels spinning smoothly on the tile. Tall, dark, and extremely handsome, he could be a model or an actor. *Italian, maybe?* His dark curls, cut short, still managed to show their wild nature. His full lips were surrounded by a shadow of short stubble that held the promise of a full beard if he let it grow. What caught and held her attention were his deep, dark eyes which called to her; a black void that she could lose herself into. "Excuse me?" she asked.

"The flight; it'll be fine. You don't have to worry 'bout it," he answered, the words infused with a light accent. Casually, he put his hands in his pants pockets. The move pushed the jacket he wore aside, causing her gaze to trail downward over his neck and lower to the broad chest he'd just accentuated. The top two buttons of his white shirt were undone and her gaze focused on the olive skin revealed there. Seconds passed before her attention bounced back to his dark eyes.

"I'm not worried about the flight," she said, shaking her head lightly, both to negate his words and to shake some sense into herself. Though why she'd bothered to respond at all, she didn't know. It must be the salesperson in her. After so many years as a real estate agent, politeness and charm had become second nature.

"You sure?" A dark, thick brow went up in question. "You seem a tad unsettled," he challenged. His eyes roamed over her face as if he was looking for something before they locked on hers. The stare seemed to go right through her. If anything, *he* was making her unsettled.

Sharon gave him a slight head tilt and a smile. "I'm not unsettled," she told him, though the more she stayed in his presence, the more flustered she became. Despite being gorgeous, something about him was off-putting and made her uncomfortable. She wished she knew what. "Have a good flight." She gave him a curt nod and another smile before she made to step around him.

"Statistically speaking, you're in great hands." He took a sidestep back allowing her to pass but continued talking, probably knowing that his words would stop her from walking away. "This airline has a clean record; no crashes at'all." The last two words blended to sound like one.

It worked; her curiosity was piqued. With a frown, she looked back at him and echoed his words. "No crashes." A nervous chuckle escaped her and she brushed her hair over her ear again, even though it hadn't moved. "That's good to know."

VICTORIAN SURPRISE

"Yup," he grinned at her, his bright white teeth contrasted against his sun-kissed skin. He tilted his head slightly and a curl landed in the middle of his forehead. "This flight will probably have a few bumps due to the turbulence from the storm, but I'm sure the plane will land without issue."

Whatever else might have been said was swallowed by the booming voice coming from the loudspeaker. Sharon jumped slightly in surprise, and her heart skipped a beat. The voice announced that her flight was now boarding and without another glance in his direction, she walked away. Quickly, she joined her family who were gathering their bags and grabbed hers, too. She didn't bother to glance at the stranger again.

Strange Flight

At her request, she'd been assigned a window seat. It was either that or sit with her siblings again—with her luck, probably between them—and she hadn't wanted to be exposed to the additional PDA she knew was coming.

Her wish had been granted, but the price was to sit next to the odd Brit. At least she thought he was British; his accent wasn't so pronounced that she could tell for sure. It didn't sound right. Sexy or not, he was an odd duck. She hadn't bothered to glance back at the gorgeous man she'd met at the terminal, yet somehow, he'd managed to sit beside her on the plane. Sharon fixated her attention on the runway as the rain began and wondered what she was going to do for the next couple of hours. Ignore him and his ramblings? Or listen with fake interest? Still wondering what to do, she chanced a quick look in his direction.

"'Ello, love," he said with an easy grin when she finally made eye contact with him.

Sharon smiled in response but didn't reply. Her stomach had taken a sudden roll, so she quickly averted her gaze back to the rain outside in an attempt to avoid additional conversation. She heard him pull out what sounded like a magazine from the pocket of the seat in front of him and sighed with relief. Perhaps now he'd let her be.

What was it about him that set her on edge? He hadn't said anything spectacularly strange, just that the airline had a clean record. If anything, that should have set her at ease. No, she thought, it wasn't his words or his mannerism that put her off. So what was making her stomach turn and her heart beat a little quicker? Because it *was* beating a little faster than usual.

It was beyond strange. Sharon was a real estate agent; she was used to meeting strangers—it came with the job. Though most transactions happened with couples, there were many that were handled by a single man or woman. She had plenty of experience meeting men for the first time at vacant properties. Probably unwise to go alone, she acknowledged, but it had never stopped her from doing what needed to be done to close the deal. Men, women, children, it didn't matter. Sharon was comfortable with anyone and everyone. *Except this one. Why?*

Sneaking a sideways glance at the stranger, she tried to look at him without giving herself away by turning. His profile was just as striking. Her scan took in his straight nose, high cheekbones, and the strong, scruffy jaw. Her gaze stopped to focus on his mouth, and she bit her lower lip when she realized that she wanted to kiss him. Shocked at the thought, she turned to face the window again.

"Get your fill already?" His voice hinted at humor.

Shit! Shit! Shit! Would he believe her if she feigned innocence? Maybe she could pretend that she hadn't been staring at him. She spun to look at him and asked calmly, "Excuse me?"

Though he held a magazine open in front of him, his black eyes locked on hers. "If you'd like," he said, the side of his mouth rising just a bit, "we could take a pic, yeah?"

Did he just ask her if she wanted a picture of him? He was being smart with her: *a picture lasts forever.* Well, she wasn't going to admit to anything. She forced a frown. "What are you talking about? A pic of what?"

"Of you and me." He flashed her a big grin, showing bright sparkling teeth. "A selfie." Without giving her an opportunity to speak, he said, "I bet a pic of us together would be brilliant." He had the nerve to wink at her.

What kind of man offered to take a selfie with a stranger? Her imagination ran wild. Sharon imagined what they would look like next to each other, her pale skin and hair against his darker tone and black curls. They would probably look amazing together. Still, that's not what strangers did. "Why would I want that?"

"I don't know. You're the one staring, love." A low, deep rumble of laughter followed his words.

"Am not!" Sharon denied quickly while tucking her hair again. She could have admitted to it, and had it been anyone else on the planet, she probably would have. But for some strange reason, this man took away her ability to think clearly. She had no idea why.

"Yeah, you are," he said as he put the magazine back into the pocket of the seat in front of him. "But it's all right. I don't mind." His wide grin remained and she got the impression that he was thoroughly enjoying her discomfort.

"Used to people staring, are you?" she asked while raising a brow. "How modest."

Once again, whatever he might have said was interrupted, this time by the flight attendant who was explaining emergency procedures, and they both turned forward to listen. Relieved, Sharon focused on the instructions—not because she wanted to know where the exits were, but because she couldn't deal with the intensity of his gaze any longer. Never before had she seen eyes so black—it was like looking into a pool of infinity.

A nervous giggle escaped her at the thought. *A pool of infinity? What's wrong with you?* Sharon didn't know if she was reverting to her sixteen-year-old self, the one who had a crush on the cutest boy in school, or if she was becoming a celibate poet. Probably the latter. Considering how long it'd been since she'd been intimate with a man, it'd only make sense.

Either way, she now had a reason for her uneasiness. His dark gaze was so intense that she felt completely exposed; like he saw everything about her—all her secrets, all her fears. She couldn't take it anymore.

They remained quiet for a long while after the attendant finished speaking. Seats were straightened to their upright position and belts were buckled while Sharon's fear renewed with the realization that the plane was about to take off. She began to grip the armrests until her knuckles were white with tension. The plane was cruising on the runway when she felt his hand cover hers. Surprised at the contact, her gaze flew to his, but his eyes were closed, a relaxed smile on his face.

For a quick moment, she considered pulling back but then reconsidered it. Despite the lie she had told him, she *was* terrified of flying. Her heart was pounding; her stomach was turning; her palms were sweaty with nerves. She was gripping the armrest so tightly, she was surprised it hadn't broken yet.

What harm would come from his small gesture? If nothing else, her attention had refocused to the touch of his hand on hers. She noticed the warmth of his skin as it penetrated her icy fingers, how small and dainty her hand felt compared to his larger one, and how her pale skin contrasted against his darker tone.

Accepting the comfort he offered, she opened her fingers and allowed his to lace through hers. This stranger might be an odd duck but right now, he was here, and he was comforting her.

Twenty Questions

Despite the weather, the take-off was uneventful. Jon wished he had brought some gum to help with the ear popping, but he had been in a bit of a hurry. He was sure it wasn't the only thing he forgot to bring with him, but whatever else he might need could be bought where he was going. After all, he was heading to Vegas, not to a deserted island.

Gentle tugging at his hand pulled his attention; his neighbor was pulling her hand back. He opened his eyes to look at her, but she was looking down at her lap. The platinum blonde curtain of her hair blocked the view of her face but it would be some time before he forgot what she looked like—porcelain skin with sky blue eyes and bright, red lips. And fingers like little icicles.

Jon was surprised she hadn't pulled back earlier. She didn't want to admit that she was afraid, but it didn't take a professional to notice. Back at the terminal, she had been jittery in her seat, tapping the soles of her high heels on the tile—when she wasn't pacing, that is. Even now, her left leg was shaking. He didn't know what was going on with her, but he was going to find out. He hoped that it was just fear of flying that she was hiding, and not something more dangerous.

"Business or pleasure?" he asked and watched as she jumped in her chair, spinning to face him with wide eyes.

"Excuse me?" she asked while sweeping her hair behind her ear with a perfectly manicured hand.

Jon was beginning to wonder if that was her catchphrase. Ignoring that, he clarified. "The reason for the flight. Why are you going to Vegas?" He gave her that charming smile that he'd used on the fairer sex since he'd discovered its effectiveness when he'd been thirteen. It hadn't failed him yet. Though when she turned to face the window again, he reconsidered. Maybe she was a lesbian. All the charm in the world wouldn't work if he didn't have the proper plumbing for her. But she had been staring at him earlier, he mused. It had to be a good sign in his favor.

Turning once again to face him, she smiled politely and asked, "Listen, honey, would you mind if we skipped the chat in favor of a quiet flight?"

At that moment, Jon realized that she was also skilled in charm. He doubted that anyone ever said no to the feminine wiles she was using on him: with a gentle touch on his forearm, she eyed him from beneath lowered lashes and curled her full lips in a sweet smile. It wouldn't work on him, but he could appreciate the skill.

"Aw, come now." He leaned a little closer to her and watched as she backed up in her seat, maintaining the distance between them. "The flight would be far more pleasant with good company." He emphasized the accent he'd picked up in the United Kingdom over the years knowing most females loved it, young and old. "Tell you what, you don't have to share any personal information, if it makes you uneasy." He wanted to sound understanding, but he needed her to talk. "How about we play twenty questions? Nothing of a personal nature; just something to help pass the time. What do you say?" He watched as her eyes flickered over his face and landed on his lips—and stayed. *So, not a lesbian.* That made him grin. "Jonathan Rossi." He stuck his hand out for a shake. "Or Jon for short."

There was a moment of hesitation before her frigid fingers wrapped around his. "Shae." After a quick second, she pulled her hand back but not before she shook his firmly. He appreciated that she wasn't a timid fish. "It's nice to meet you."

"Charmed, I'm sure." He straightened in his seat though his gaze remained on her. "Well, Shae, will you be so kind as to play with me?"

She considered it and then gave a slight shrug. "Sure, why not?"

"Brilliant," he beamed at her. "Would you care to go first or shall I?" Before she had a chance to respond, he said, "Though I must say, I've been taught that ladies should always go first. I will, however, defer to your preference since you'll be doing me a favor."

Giving him a sideways glance, she asked, "When you say 'go first,' do you mean I get to ask questions first? Or answer them? Because that could mean a world of difference."

"Whatever your pleasure," he replied quickly. Over the years, Jon had learned that most people loved talking about themselves. There was a basic human need to feel important to someone else; the need to feel valued, to be *interesting* to another. As long as someone was listening, then the chatter would continue, sometimes to the point of revealing secrets unexpectedly. For some, however, the opposite held true. Some were curious and wanted to know everything about the person they were with and divulged nothing about themselves. Jon wondered what category she would fit into.

Shae tilted her head sideways a bit before admitting her thoughts. "Well... You are intriguing, in a car-wreck kind of way. I'd love to know what part of the world created such an oddity like yourself." Decision made, she gave him her first real smile. It was blindingly beautiful. Exquisite. "Though I can't imagine this game will take very long. Your accent gives you away."

She's a sharp one. Jon chuckled. "You might be surprised." He watched as a curious frown crossed her brow.

"You're not from the UK?" she asked, eyes scrunched thoughtfully.

Playing along, Jon bobbed his head noncommittally. "You need to clarify the question. Am I from the UK, as in: was I *born* there? Or, am I from the UK, as in: this most recent trip? Or do you mean: do I currently reside there?"

Her soft laugh was musical, endearing, and her eyes sparkled with humor. "What are you? A lawyer?"

"I will count that as your first question," Jon told her. "The answer is no, I am not a lawyer." He leaned just an inch closer to her before continuing. "Though I can assure you, there are plenty of lawyers around the world, including the UK. Ready for question two?" It was a good sign that she didn't back away again.

There was a pause as she considered the next one. "Okay, were you born in the UK?"

"No," he said simply. "Three?"

Thinking out loud, she mumbled, "Obviously, you've been there. Unless you got your accent from another area where they speak with that accent." She bit her bottom lip briefly before asking, "Have you ever been there?" He wanted to kiss it and make it better.

"Yes. Four?"

VICTORIAN SURPRISE

"Where were you born?" Shae asked outright.

It was his turn to laugh. "That's not how twenty questions work, love." He watched as her gaze dropped to his lips again and wondered if she was imagining just how good a kiss would be. Because he'd certainly pondered how those plump red lips would feel against his. He leaned toward her just a bit and whispered his next words, forcing her to come closer to hear them. "The idea is to make it last, for as long as we can, before reaching the inevitable conclusion. The pleasure comes from prolonging the experience," her eyes shot up to lock with his, "for as long as we possibly can." His knowing smile was slow, deliberate, and it pleased him to notice that her gaze dropped to watch. "What is question four?"

After a barely perceptible shake of her head, her eyes met his. "I'm sorry, I'm not used to having time to kill. For the past several years, I've been on the run, constantly going from one thing to another without a break, and this feels strange. I'm more accustomed to getting to the end as efficiently as possible. And not taking the time to enjoy anything by…" The slow rise of her lips became sultry as she finished softly, "prolonging it, as you put it."

Ignoring the tempting smile, he focused on the words she had used. They caught and held his attention. "On the run?" Though his detective instincts being on high alert, his voice remained cool, showing just enough interest to keep her talking. "Care to share?" Jon studied her face, scrutinizing every micro-expression she revealed; but there wasn't much. She maintained appropriate eye contact; she didn't fidget, didn't pull away. Either she was very good at hiding things, or there was nothing to hide.

"It's just work." With a dismissive wave of her hand, she continued, "Boring, boring crap. Nothing you'd want to hear about."

It was time to up his game. Slowly, he shrank the distance between them again, drawing them into closer, more intimate, proximity. Locking eyes with her, he murmured, "I don't believe there is anything about you that I don't want to know, Shae."

Another soft laugh filled the air and she shook her head. "You're quite the flirt, Jon." Still, she looked at him from beneath lowered lashes, a playful smile on her lips. She was enjoying the attention.

"Possibly," he teased, "but it's the truth." She looked away from him briefly. He studied her every move, watched as she brushed her hair from her face, the red nail polish catching the light. He monitored her breathing, looked for nervous tics, or micro-expressions that didn't match the words, all the while believing she was just nervous about the flight. He certainly hoped that was the truth.

With a low chuckle, she said, "If there's enough time, you can ask your twenty questions. I'm not sure you'll be able to learn everything about me before the plane lands but, as you said, it'll help pass the time." She pursed her lips thoughtfully. "So, question four."

Blue Black

"So how did you get a British accent if you were born in New York?" Sharon asked him. It had taken nineteen questions to finally get there, but she got her answer. Jon was very relaxed and looking absolutely edible next to her. Between the deep timbre of his voice and the delicious foreign accent, he was getting sexier by the minute and she wanted to keep him talking for as long as she could. She was utterly taken with him.

"During my travels, I met an MMA specialist who lives just outside London. I spent years there, training with him."

"Wait, you're a mixed martial arts fighter?" Sharon had met a lot of people as a real estate agent, but never an MMA fighter. An image of what he'd look like bare-chested flickered through her imagination; she nearly drooled.

"Not quite," he grinned. "Though I've been in many fights, my intention is to open a dojo and teach self-defense. This way, I get to keep most of my marbles."

"Nice." She nodded in approval. "I get the impression that you haven't started. Why not?"

"I haven't found the right place yet. There are a couple of locations that would work but I'm still looking."

"Oh." Another opportunity landing in her lap. *Do I want to go there?* Sharon quickly replied to her mental question. *Yes, anything to be around him.* "Are you working with a real estate agent?"

"Nah, I don't need one." He shook his head.

Sharon had heard that line, many times. She didn't understand why people would prefer to do all the work themselves when they could get help from a professional for nothing. Since the listing party typically paid for both sides, why wouldn't *everyone* get help? And though it was true that there were a lot of sites that listed properties, there was a lot of inside information that those sites didn't contain; for example, when a property was under agreement already. But she wouldn't argue with him about it. "Well, honey, if you change your mind, you should call me. I can help."

With a rueful grin, he laughed, and she caught her breath. Even his laughter was amazing, coming from deep within him.

"You're a real estate agent."

It was a statement, not a question, but she felt she needed to confirm. "Yup. Started right out of high school and I've been running nonstop ever since." And, boy, was she tired of it.

"Do you like it?" Jon asked.

The typical response formed quickly, *Yes, I love it,* but for some reason, she didn't feel like giving him her standard lie. "At one time, yes…" Her words trailed off. It was bad form to tell a potential client that her love for the industry had faded long ago. Successful real estate agents were immaculate actors. Everything could be falling apart but they'd always smile, because in front of a client, everything would always be *perfect.* Always. Rather than complaining or lying, she said nothing more.

Jon finished for her, "But not any longer." His gaze was focused solely on her. It was so intense, it made her want to squirm.

VICTORIAN SURPRISE

Sharon sighed and shook her head. "I'm very boring. I'd much rather discuss your plans for your dojo. Where are you looking?"

Once again, he surprised her by covering her hand with his. Sincerity infused his deep voice when he said, "There is nothing about you that I don't want to know, no matter how boring it is, as you put it."

She tried to laugh it off but all of a sudden, the plane jerked unexpectedly. Her eyes grew round as her heart skipped a beat and her stomach dropped in terror.

"Hey, it's okay. It's just a little turbulence." This time, there was a soothing quality to his words, as if he was speaking to a skittish mare.

Nervous laughter escaped her at the thought. *I am skittish.* Staring out of the window, her panic induced laughter grew as turbulence struck again. Though she was aware that *technically* they were far away, she saw bolts of lightning brightening the night sky and wondered what would happen if they hit the plane. Her stomach rolled and she gripped his hand for dear life.

"Look at me, Shae." The words came to her but seemed so far away. "Shae." More persistent, someone called to her, "Look at me." Sharon noticed that there was tugging at her hand, and she looked down at it, surprised to see it wrapped in a masculine claps. "Up here, love."

Sharon's eyes locked with Jon's, and she stared at the same black void she had noticed earlier. Pools of darkness, she had thought, encircled by thick, curling lashes. *Women would pay dearly to have those*, she considered with a giggle. "You are so beautiful," she commented before her usual filter stopped her. Another burst of nervous giggles was cut abruptly when the plane suddenly dropped, making her feel like she had nothing solid beneath her.

Distracting her again, Jon gave her a lopsided grin and his eyes beamed at her, though his expression was filled with concern. "The feeling is mutual, love."

The intensity of his gaze was too much and she looked away.

Immediately, he called her attention back. "Look at me. Focus on me."

Sharon had no idea how much time passed while they stared into each other's eyes. It might have been a minute; it might have been five hours. Time lost meaning as she saw only the solid black irises, an incredible void. *Infinity,* she thought again.

But the time did pass, and eventually, Sharon noticed the plane had settled into a steady flight again. Taking a deep breath, she straightened in her seat. *How embarrassing...*

"You okay, love?" Still worried about her, Jon frowned.

Sharon laughed lightly and nodded. "Yeah, I'm fine." She pulled her hand back. Immediately, she missed the warmth of his reassuring touch. Avoiding his watchful gaze, she finally admitted, "In case you haven't noticed, I really don't like flying." His low laugh pulled her eyes back to him.

Jon gave her an exaggerated frown of mock confusion and said, "No, I hadn't noticed at'all. I was only staring because you have the most stunning blue eyes I've ever seen. Did you know they're almost crystal cut? With little flexes of lighter blue scattered throughout? They are quite lovely."

The corners of her lips rose in relief. He wasn't going to make a big deal out of it. "Thank you." She

VICTORIAN SURPRISE

sucked her lower lip in for a second, biting it. "Yours are also stunning. I've never seen eyes so black, so devoid of any other color."

"Thank you. They were a birthday gift." He winked at her. "Now, where were we before we became lost in each other, hmm?"

Sharon tried to remember what they'd been speaking about before nature tried to kill them. "Your dojo," she said just as he spoke, their words overlapping.

"Real estate," he said.

Unspoken Dreams

"So, why has real estate lost its sparkle?" Jon pressed. He hadn't been lying when he'd said he wanted to know everything about her. At first, because she'd been fidgety and he'd needed to know the cause. Now that he was certain it was due to the flight itself, he was simply curious about her. And chatting did make travel easier to bear.

Jon watched as she shook her head. Shae didn't like to share things and he wondered why. Most people loved to talk about themselves. What had happened to make her so guarded? "Oh, come now. I've shared with you," he insisted.

She shook her head and spoke softly, "Successful real estate agents don't complain. They smile; they pay attention to their clients; they pay attention to what is spoken and especially what *isn't* spoken. But most importantly, they're agreeable. Everything is perfect. Always." Her full lips pressed tightly for a moment before she continued. "To say otherwise is... reckless."

"I'm not your client, Shae. And whatever you say will stay solely between us." He gave her a playful grin. "After all, we are headed to Vegas. And you know what happens in Vegas..." His voice trailed off.

She chuckled, "Stays in Vegas. So I've heard."

"Exactly," he said triumphantly.

"Jon, honey," her voice lost the laughter when she continued, "everyone I meet is a potential client. And even if we never do a transaction together, there's still the possibility of a referral. My reputation is everything. It's imperative that everyone I meet views me as a professional, always."

"Understandable," he said, "but being a professional doesn't mean you're a robot. Even when you love your career, there's nothing wrong with not loving all aspects of the industry. I can assure you, there are moments when I don't love what I do; when I want to throttle my clients for being dimwits." They both laughed softly and he wondered if it was enough for her to open up to him. "So what parts don't you love about it?" For a brief moment, she worried her bottom lip and he wondered if she would say anything. When her pink tongue darted out to soothe her lips, he was tempted to kiss them and make it all better. When she sighed deeply, he knew she'd given up.

"There is no down time," she said ruefully. "It's exhausting. My phone rings all day long and into the night. If it's not a call, then it's a text, or an email. People don't care that it's midnight and you're most likely sleeping. Some expect you to respond immediately.

"My personal favorite," Shae continued, her voice a blend of anger and exhaustion, "was when a couple refused to reply to their mortgage broker. Time and again, he tried to get necessary documents from them. Two weeks before the closing, I called to inform them that they'd lost the house because I couldn't get a commitment letter from the bank. At that point, they expected me to drop everything – and all of my *other* clients – so I could help them fix it." She shook her head. "Because the world revolved around them."

"I'm sorry," Jon offered softly. "Surely, they're not all like that, are they?"

This time, her laugh was hollow. "No. On occasion, there's the broken heating system, or the mold in the basement, or the leaky roof, that I'm to blame for." She shrugged resignedly. "After all, I'm the realtor and should know all of these things. And should have advised them ahead of time, because I know *everything* about a property. No," she quickly corrected herself, "because I know *everything* about *all* properties, whether I list them or not."

Jon got the impression that she didn't speak about her job often; not like this. While she spoke, Shae's voice lowered with bitterness, her lips flattened, and her brow furrowed in frustration. He had no doubt her words were true. He remained quiet and allowed her to vent.

"And I should be psychic and know that the heating system will break in a couple of years; or that the big tree in the yard had roots that had grown into the foundation." She turned to him, and her eyes narrowed to slits. "Do you know what the worst part about all of this is?"

Not knowing what to say, he simply shook his head.

"The inspection reports usually list the items homebuyers should review more carefully. They are given the tools, but most ignore them and blame someone else." She shook her head and sighed. "I'm so tired of it. So tired of *all* of it."

Before Jon had an opportunity to respond, the pilot's voice came through the speakers. They were preparing to land.

Turning back to her, he asked, "I'm sure you've considered this but why haven't you moved on? What holds you back from pursuing another career?"

Shae shrugged. "It's all I've ever done. It's all I know how to do."

Rejecting her words, he shook his head. "Nah. Just because you've never done anything else doesn't mean that's *all* you know how to do." He paused. "What is your passion? What do you *love* to do, Shae?"

Crinkles appeared on her forehead as she considered his questions. She worried her bottom lip again and he wondered if she was going to voice her thoughts or just ignore them. Eventually, the look in her eyes softened, as did her tone when she finally spoke. "When I was a kid, I loved to draw."

"Oh? You're an artist at heart?" he pursued.

"No, I mean architectural designs. My dad used to design houses and I loved to watch him draw." She shrugged again. "I once thought that's what I would have done, too."

"What went wrong?"

"My parents needed help in the real estate office," she said simply. "At first, I helped with the little things around the office, answering phones and making appointments. But it wasn't long before my dad pushed me to get my license so I could help with everything."

"It's not too late to follow your dream," Jon pointed out. "It's never too late."

"Okay, mister motivational speaker," Shae joked with him, "if you say so."

Her indulgent grin faded from her face as the descent began. Worry darkened her gaze as her eyes went round, and when Jon offered her his hand, she took it without comment. Lacing their fingers together, she faced forward as if she was awaiting execution, and held tightly.

To fill the silence, and to distract her as best as he could, Jon told her a story from his childhood, a misadventure involving mac and cheese and his best mate at the time. And what happens to boxed mac and cheese when the directions aren't followed, and someone forgets to add the milk.

Though her icy fingers held onto his like a lifeline, gripping so tightly that they were white, Jon was thrilled each time she let out a soft laugh or shook her head at his childish ignorance. He heard her sigh of relief as the tires rolled onto the runway, and when he felt the vice grip loosen, he was tempted to make a joke about his numb fingers. Instead, he commented, "I never did find out why you were headed to Vegas."

With an easy smile, she motioned to one of the couples who accompanied her on the trip. "My brother's fiancée wants a quick wedding."

"Oh, brilliant," he said quickly. He leaned toward her again and in a conspirator's voice, he whispered, "Is she knocked up?"

Playfully, she smacked his firm bicep. "No!" Laughing, and in a low voice to mirror his, she continued, "Sam's worried he'll change his mind."

Jon looked over at the couples she'd been sitting with in the airport and noticed the pair without wedding bands. Despite her words, it was clear that there was no danger of a breakup. Her brother's eyes left his fiancée's only for short moments, and when he looked back, there was a light there. A playful smile touched his lips while he listened intently to whatever she was saying. And even if he wasn't looking, a possessive hand was always on her leg. Those two were very much in love. "I can see why she's worried." With a nod, he continued , "Your brother is definitely a flight risk." Shae's soft laugh pulled at him and he faced her, noting how her eyes lit up and her full lips rose just a bit higher on the left side when she grinned. *Damn, she's gorgeous.* "Will I see you again?"

The question startled her and her eyes went wide again. He prepared himself for a polite negative when her grin softened into a small smile. Thoughtfully, she gave him a sideways glance and bit her full, bottom lip. And when the reply came, it was his turn to be surprised. "Anything is possible in Vegas."

Hesitant Departure

As people stood and began pulling bags from the overhead compartments, the noise around them made further talk difficult. Everyone seemed to be in a hurry to get off the plane except maybe the two of them. They stayed where they were, seeming hesitant to leave. Sharon certainly was.

All of a sudden, Scott leaned in from the empty seat in front of them. "Are you coming?"

"Yes," she said and stood up. So much for prolonging the inevitable. Looking back, she said, "Thank you, Jon, for making this flight... almost enjoyable." When she first got on, she had thought him to be odd, and she still did, a little. But he had helped her get through the flight, and she would be forever grateful for that. If only he could be around for the trip back.

Also standing, he asked with a tilt of his head, "Almost?"

Sharon shrugged and smiled up at him. "It was still a flight."

Jon shook his head and said, "Pleasure was mine, to be sure." *Goodness, that accent was sexy!*

She had expected him to step out into the aisle, but when he didn't go any farther, she worked around him. Awkwardly, she raised a long leg to the other side of his two and for a fleeting second, she straddled him. During the move, she lost her balance and had to grip his shoulders to keep herself upright. Their positions were suddenly very intimate. Her heart began to pound, not from fear but from the thrill of him.

Her breasts were pressed against his hard chest, and she felt the now familiar warmth of his hand on her back, pulling her closer. It would be so easy to raise her face to his and plant a quick kiss on him, just a taste, as she had been tempted to do earlier. Sharon's gaze settled on his mouth. Running her tongue over her lips, she wondered how his would feel on her own, whether his stubble would feel rough against her cheek. Her belly spun with anticipation as she allowed herself to spiral into his allure.

"Hey," Sammy's sharp voice intruded on her daydream. "You gonna let my sister go, or what?"

Sharon almost groaned aloud at the interruption. "Coming!" she snapped in irritation. Forcing herself away from Jon, she scrambled over him into the aisle and turned to see the four people currently staring at her. It was then that Sharon realized the plane was almost empty.

"I'll be out in a minute. I need my bag." Waving her right hand dismissively, Sharon shooed at them to leave, "No, really, feel free to go." When they still didn't move, she bit out, "Go!"

The two women looked at each other with knowing grins and walked away. Sharon's siblings, however, didn't follow but kept staring at Jon while he pulled her bag from the overhead compartment. Their identical frowns were almost comical.

Ignoring them, he handed the bag to her with a smile. When she had it in hand, she murmured softly to him, "Thank you."

"You're welcome," Jon whispered in response.

Thankfully, he was completely unperturbed by the death looks he was getting from her brothers and went about his business casually. As he pulled his own bag down, along with his jacket, Sharon admired his perfect T shape, wide shoulders, lean hips. He moved with such athletic grace. She stared guilelessly at his firm butt and imagined his abs were just as tight. If drooling in public were acceptable, she'd be doing it now.

"Shae?" Scott called again. At least his tone was slightly less annoying than Sammy's.

"Give me a minute. Goodness!" Sharon fished for a business card and handed it to Jon as soon as he turned around. "In case you change your mind about an agent." She turned to walk away but gave him a beguiling look over her shoulder. "I don't bite."

Jon watched her as he put the card in an inside pocket of his jacket. With an easy grin, he replied, "I'll keep that in mind."

Overprotective Brothers

Typical overprotective brothers, Jon mused with humor as he watched the family walk away.

Manners dictated that he step out into the aisle or at least lean back to give her as much room as possible while she passed, but temptation won over and he used the lack of space to force contact instead. She was such a striking beauty, and they had spent so much time chatting, he hadn't wanted them to part ways just yet, at least not before he experienced her full breasts against him. Pulling her body to his as she struggled to past him and into the aisle was just wicked. Hell, he'd been tempted to give her a goodbye kiss, to taste her lips, to sweep his tongue through her mouth. He quickly reconsidered when he remembered her two siblings were still watching him like hawks.

As he walked after them, he kept some distance between them, lest the brothers get the idea to turn around and try to punch him for the cheap feel. He laughed at the thought. After all the years he spent training to get his sixth-degree black belt, and title of Master, if these two landed a punch, Jon would have to consider a new career.

He couldn't blame them, though. If he had a sister as beautiful as Shae, he would be overprotective, too. Following them through the terminal, he watched the sway of her hips and appreciated the grace of her movements. *Yes, he would definitely want to protect her.*

Lena Lane

As they walked, her brothers took up protective positions on either side of her, their significant others beside them. She seemed oblivious to it, though. At some point, she had grabbed her phone and was looking at it as they strode forward, the five of them walking side by side as a unit. *Must be nice, having such a group to look out for you.*

He shook the thought away and pulled out his own phone. He had things to do.

Unexpected Texts

Sharon was afraid to look out the window; her room was so high. *God, I hate heights.* Unfortunately, the only way to make the incredible view go away was to close the curtains. And to do that, she'd have to get very close to the windows. She swore under her breath.

Ignoring her pounding heart, she practically ran to grab the rod and drew the curtain shut, groaning when she realized it only went halfway. In a flurry, she ran to the other side and repeated the action, breathing a sigh of relief when the threat of falling to her death was no longer imminent. Amazing what a piece of cloth could do.

At Samantha's request, they all got full suites on the upper floors because she wanted to see as much of the strip as she could from her room. Sharon had tried to get a room closer to the ground, but Samantha had asked that they stay close together. Considering what she'd gone through, losing her family so young, Sharon hadn't had the heart to say no. After all, both Scott and Sharon had adopted Samantha into the family as one of their own. And if Samantha wanted to see the entire strip from her room, then Samantha would get her wish, but Sharon had to promptly close the blinds as soon as she walked in.

Pulling out her laptop, she sat at the desk of her suite and immediately got to work. The others may be on vacation, but she had to stay focused. The beauty of modern technology included the ability to still service her clients, even while thousands of miles away. She was responding to her third email when her phone vibrated with an incoming text. Sharon sighed. *If it's not an email, it's a text or a call.* Annoyed, she finished typing her thought before she looked at it.

Do you never bite? The message was from an unknown number, but she had an idea who it might be, and her heart began to pound in her chest. A second message quickly followed, *What if I asked nicely?*

Sharon nibbled her lower lip even as she grinned. *Anything is possible under the right circumstances.* Send. For Jon, she would make all kinds of exceptions. She'd bite, nibble, lick, suck, and kiss any place he wanted.

On the way to the hotel, she had replayed their conversation from the plane and had really hoped to see him again. He was sexy, funny, sweet. Quite the perfect combination of temptation in a man. But once she had arrived at the hotel, she decided to let him go. After all, she couldn't keep wasting time on someone she would probably never see again. More importantly, she still had a lot of work to do, even if she wasn't at home.

Distracted, she put her phone down and tried to finish her email. She had to read it three times before the words made any sense to her. Making a couple of quick corrections, she sent it. Just at the right time, apparently, since her phone vibrated with another incoming message. Her heart thumped in her chest as she grabbed it.

And what would those circumstances be?

Holding the phone in her hand, she looked at the other fifteen new emails waiting in her box and contemplated which to address first: the gorgeous man texting her or her clients? Her responsibility to her

VICTORIAN SURPRISE

clients pulled at her. Her reputation as an agent was at stake, as was her family's. But wasn't some downtime necessary in order to have a balanced life? Why couldn't she have a life outside of work? One where she wouldn't have to chat about offers and inspections during her non-existent dates?

Sharon's fingers flew over the screen of her phone. *For one, it'd depend on who was getting bitten.* Send.

Pretending to focus on her work, she put the phone back down and looked at her emails. Filtering by the subject line, she clicked on what she assumed was an easy one, but she didn't get a chance to read it before her phone went off again.

How about someone with stunning eyes?

Feeling like she was back in high school, she replied, *How stunning are they? Are we talking about baby blues? Or maybe forest green? Hazel eyes can be quite stunning too.* Send.

At that point, she gave up on work altogether and shut her laptop down. Even if she wasn't distracted by the incoming texts, she would be playing their conversation in her head again. She knew that the rest of the night would include some fantasies.

I believe you described them as stunningly black, devoid of color.

They were quite stunning. Sharon flashed back to her earlier musings, and remembered that they were so dark, they appeared to be a deep void, like pools of infinity. *What? I said that? I don't remember it.* Send.

Then perhaps you need to see them again.

Was that an invitation to meet him? Her heart skipped a beat before speeding up. *Perhaps I do. What do you suggest?*

The question came through quickly, *Have you had dinner?*

Lena Lane

She wanted nothing more than to go to dinner with him but it was already late, and she had to be up and ready for a wedding early in the morning. After all, as the maid of honor, it was her job to make sure everything went smoothly. It would be wise to decline, but she was tired of being the responsible one. Besides, wasn't that what caffeine was for? *It's a little late for dinner. How about a midnight snack instead?* Send.

Whatever your pleasure.

Hi Honey

Just as she'd told him, Shae was standing by one of the slot machines at the entrance, occasionally clicking the spinner. Jon slowed his pace to appreciate her profile. His memory hadn't been playing tricks on him; she really was gorgeous. Her hair wasn't bound but tucked behind her ear again. She was wearing a flowing dress that ended right before her knees in the front but reached her ankles in the back. She had made a wise choice in her shoes; just a little heel. They would be perfect for a walk.

As he crossed the room, his gaze swept through the area (old habits were hard to break) and saw several men—and a few women—eyeing her. He wasn't the only one appreciating her beauty.

Still at a distance, Jon watched as one of the men approached her. He beamed a grin at her, and she smiled back. Some words were exchanged and Jon saw her shake her head. Unfazed by her refusal, the man reached out to stroke her bare arm. Her smile faded as she quickly stepped back to break contact. It didn't take much longer for Jon's hurried steps to reach her after that. Whatever the man wanted, Shae wanted no part of it.

Seeing Jon approach, Shae's face broke into a relieved smile. He never felt so good about coming to someone's rescue. As soon as he was within earshot, she called out, "Hi, honey."

Jon quickly deduced that she had told the stranger she was waiting for her... husband? Boyfriend? It didn't matter. Playing along, he replied, "Sorry I'm late, sweets." He leaned in and gave her a quick peck on the lips. He would have loved to enjoy a longer kiss, but this was just for show. Next time, he'd savor her lips more deeply.

When they pulled apart, he wrapped an arm around her shoulders and pulled her close to his side, acting the part of a possessive lover. It felt completely natural. If she was his, that's what he'd do. Her small hand landing on his chest told the world they were a tight couple. Giving the man a scowl, Jon asked, "Who's this?"

"No one of importance," the stranger said. "Just wanted to keep the lady company while she waited." The smile he gave them was cold and never reached his eyes. "You guys have a great night." At that point, he turned and walked away.

Shae turned to Jon and stepped back from his embrace. Shaking her head with a frown, she said, "I'm sorry about that. He was a little strange, and it was the first thing that came to mind."

"It's all right, love," Jon grinned. "I have no problems being called your honey." It was true.

She chuckled with a shrug. "I don't understand why random, strange men keep walking up to me, thinking they can just talk me up."

"It's the price you pay for being so beautiful." He watched as she shook her head at the compliment, but appreciated that she didn't play modest and dismiss it.

"Thank you." With a smile, she met his gaze and said, "Shall we head out and forage for your snack?"

VICTORIAN SURPRISE

Noticing her choice of words, he clarified, "We don't have to get any food, if you're not interested. How about a nice walk instead?"

Her captivating blue eyes beamed at him. "Perfect."

He offered her his arm, and once she took it, they headed outside.

A Kiss

The air outside was far cooler than she would have expected for Vegas. Sharon thought about it and remembered reading something about temperatures dropping a lot at night, especially in November. She'd have to remember that in the future. Luckily, Jon's body was warm and she could snuggle up to him as they walked. Arm in arm, they strolled along for a few minutes in comfortable silence.

It was a good thing because she didn't think she was capable of witty conversation, distracted as she was by the man walking with her. She was so relieved to see Jon at the hotel when that jerk was creeping her out, she could have jumped him right then and there. The weirdo had kept making advances, and even though Sharon had told him she was waiting for someone, he had insisted that she go with him to the bar. If Jon had arrived any later, Sharon might have had to call security on the stranger.

But he had arrived at just the right time, looking sexy in his black slacks and navy button-down shirt. He had showered and shaved. When he had leaned in for their quick kiss back at the hotel, she could see his hair was still a little wet. And now, she could smell his clean and musky scent. His sexy level rose a few notches.

"Looking forward to the wedding tomorrow?" His deep voice broke the silence.

"Yes," she admitted easily. "I love seeing them so happy, and Samantha will be positively radiant." Her head bobbed a bit before she continued. "This is her vision of a perfect wedding, though we're all a little bummed Dad decided not to join us."

"Why is that?"

Giving him a sideways glance, she asked, "Why is Dad not joining us or why is this her version of a perfect wedding?"

He chuckled. "Let's begin with why Dad's not coming."

Sharon bit a sarcastic laugh. "He thinks Sam is out for my brother's money," she scoffed. "What he doesn't realize is that she has more money than all of us." After a brief paused, she added, "Combined."

"And no one has bothered to tell him?"

"He's being an ass." The words were sharp with anger, even to her own ears. She softened her tone. "He jumped to conclusions right from the start and is refusing to admit that he might have been wrong." The anger left her voice completely when she said, "Everyone can see how in love those two are." Abruptly, she turned to him and asked, "How about you? You never mentioned why you're here."

"I am here for a similar reason," he said, the deep timbre of his sexy voice resonating through her. *Goodness, what a delicious accent!* She hoped he wouldn't lose that inflection any time soon. "My best friend is getting married in three days' time."

"Aw," Sharon replied with a sweet smile. "Congratulations to them. May they have many happy years together."

"I shall share your good wishes with her in the morning."

Taken aback, she stopped walking to look at him. "Your best friend is a girl?"

"Yes," he said simply. "Is that so odd?"

Sharon shrugged. "It's just uncommon." They began walking again and she said, "More often than not, friends of the opposite sex end up together."

His laughter rumbled his chest. "Not always."

"I guess," she said simply.

"What? You don't believe men and women can be friends?" Jon challenged.

That gave her pause. She'd never really thought about it. Her romantic heart was always setting people up; everyone should have a significant other. Even if *she* couldn't get her *Happily Ever After*, she was always doing her best to make sure others did. Did she believe that made it impossible for two people to love each other without a romantic connection? "I'm not sure," Sharon answered honestly. "I am a romantic at heart; I love seeing people together." She shrugged a second time. "Friendship blossoms into love easily enough."

"Not in this case," he told her. "Though I love her dearly, we agreed we're not good for each other." Before she could ask why not, he volunteered, "It helps to note that I have extra equipment that she doesn't appreciate."

Sharon stopped walking again, confusion reflected in her furrowed brow. "Extra equipment?"

The corner of his mouth rose with humor. He leaned over and whispered softly in her ear, "I have a penis."

Understanding, she laughed. "Your best friend is a lesbian."

"A big one," he confirmed.

They resumed walking, their steps slow as they looked at the bright lights. All around them, people were talking and laughing. Like them, they were out for a late walk to take in the wonders of Vegas at night.

VICTORIAN SURPRISE

"Well, honey, I'm sure you'll find someone who will love you even more than she does," Sharon told him. "Better even."

"Well," he spoke earnestly, "love is like a rainbow. It comes in all different ways. Just because it's different from another, it doesn't mean it's any less powerful."

At those words, she pulled them to another stop. Looking at him with a hint of wonder, she said, "That is one of the most beautiful things I've ever heard." She looked into his dark eyes and saw the soul of a poet. "How is it possible that an MMA fighter can have such an open heart?"

Sarcastically, he teased, "What? A fighter can't love?"

Sharon would have worried that she'd insulted him if his eyes weren't laughing at her and lips weren't raised in a grin. Still, she was quick to negate the idea. "No, no, no," she tapped his hard chest and giggled. "I'm sure you're a wonderful lover. It's just unexpected."

He snickered. "Wouldn't you love to know first-hand."

Suddenly, the feel of the moment changed and they were no longer discussing the emotion of love, but the act. The humor left them, and her heart leapt in her ribcage as their eyes locked. Sharon took a deep breath to steady her nerves and bit her lower lip as she remembered their quick peck in the hotel. It had been too fast. "I bet I would."

Jon swept her hair back and tucked it behind her ear as she had done a thousand times. Then he caressed her cheek. The warmth of his palm against her face made her belly spin with expectation. They were standing close, so close. Time stood still while he traced her lower lip with his thumb, right before he leaned in to kiss her. Her belly dropped at the contact.

Lena Lane

The question that had plagued her since before the plane took off was answered: how would his lips feel on hers? They felt amazing. Goosebumps erupted over her body, not from the cold but from the heat of him. Gentle and sweet, his lips touched hers lightly, before the brief brush quickly turned more pressing. Once, twice, three times, their lips met and parted, each kiss becoming more urgent as their curiosity grew. Her breathing labored, and her body swayed to his, an unconscious demand to be as close to him as possible. She reached up and draped her arms around his neck, pulling him, trapping him.

He answered by wrapping his around her waist, and holding her body tightly against his own. The feel of his hard chest against hers just made her want more. She opened her mouth to him, invited him in, and was thrilled when his tongue swept through it, a quick brush that left her yearning. Out of breath, she pulled back and held his face between her hands, just long enough to confirm he was as hungry for her as she was for him. When she saw his hooded gaze, heard his labored breathing, felt his fists gripping her dress on her lower back, she knew.

Sharon pulled his face to hers and kissed him. Her lips lightly teased him, nibbled him, and then kissed him seductively. And when he gasped, it was her turn to sweep her tongue through his mouth. His met hers and together, they danced. They joined, then drifted apart, then came together again, each touch infused with even more desire. A tease that started slow and gentle, quickly grew to fast and furious. Starving, they searched for satiation that would never come solely by kissing.

Understanding the need, he demanded in a husky voice, "Come to my room."

VICTORIAN SURPRISE

Gasping, heart pounding in her chest, she looked at him and wondered what to do. She wanted to; God knows she did. Her nipples were tight and her core demanded more. But she had met him only that afternoon. It hadn't even been a full day. If she went through with this, what would it say about her?

Her lack of a quick reply seemed to be answer enough for him and he backed up. Also out of breath, he said, "No, of course not." He shook his head. "Don't know what I was thinking." Before waiting for her reply, he continued, "I'll take you back to your hotel now."

As calmly as could be, as if they hadn't just kissed each other into a lust filled frenzy, he offered her his arm again. Ignoring how her body demanded release, she hooked her arm through his, and they walked back together.

At least she wasn't cold anymore.

Screw Wise

Wow, she was amazing. Never before had he wanted to lose himself in the moment as he had just a few minutes ago. He would have loved to just keep going and have sex right there, in the middle of the Vegas strip. He doubted they'd be the first, but she wasn't some floozy to shag in the street, and after just meeting, no less. Luckily, she had enough sense for the both of them.

Her arm linked through his, they walked. Needing to break the tension in the air, he decided to break the silence. "So, tomorrow is Samantha's version of a perfect wedding. What makes a Vegas wedding perfect for her?"

"She's a bit shy and doesn't have any family, so no big venues for her. And she hates being wasteful. Extravagant shows of wealth, like expensive tablecloths or gold trimmed dinnerware, aren't for her. The most excessive thing I've ever seen from her is the choice of very pricey hotel rooms for this trip, and only because she wanted to see as much of the Vegas strip from her suite as she could." After a moment, she corrected herself. "Oh, and she splurges on a specific type of bottled water from France. Apparently, it's the best."

"Okay…" Jon mumbled. "So she likes things simple. What about you? What's your ideal wedding?"

"Aw, honey, are you planning for our union already?" she joked with him. He'd be worried if he hadn't heard the laughter in her voice. "I can't blame you. I'm quite a catch, and it's good to start early."

VICTORIAN SURPRISE

When he looked at her, she winked at him. On a more serious note, she replied, "Truthfully? I've never had the need to even consider it, so I have no idea.

"Sarah and Scott had your typical big church wedding with a couple of hundred people in attendance," she continued, "followed by the typical fancy reception, formal pictures, big cake, dancing, champagne, the whole nine yards.

"Sam and Sam want the complete opposite—to the extreme," she chuckled. "A simple, and *fast* mind you, 'I do' in Vegas. And their version of a reception will be an all-inclusive buffet dinner. Knowing Sam, coupons were probably involved."

It was his turn to pull her to a stop. Interrupting her, he asked, "Sam and Sam?"

She grinned knowingly. "Yup. Samuel Sampson is my brother. Samantha Waters is his fiancée. They both prefer to go by Sam."

"Damn," he snickered, "that must make family dinners fun." They began walking again, but before she could say anything more, he stopped. "Wait, please tell me she's taking his last name. That'd be a riot."

At that, she laughed out loud. "She plans on it, yes."

"How wicked! She sounds like such fun," *because she loves to push his buttons.* After a moment, he asked, "How does your brother feel about that?"

"Frustrated." Sharon tugged on his arm and they resumed their stroll. "But my family calls him Sammy, and that makes things a little less confusing."

"I bet."

They had reached the main entrance to the hotel and their pace slowed. Dragging out their last moments together by mutual, if unspoken, agreement, she led him to the elevator before releasing his arm.

Shae looked at him and nibbled her lower lip again, pulling his attention there. Instead of saying goodnight as he should have, he leaned in and breathed, "Your poor lips," against them. "You should be more careful, or you'll bite them off completely." As if to soothe them, he brushed his against hers gently.

What was intended to be a sweet, and quick, goodnight kiss turned ravenous in seconds. She grabbed his lapels and forced him to stay when he would've pulled back. He held her forearms and didn't know whether to push her away or pull her closer. But she kept kissing him. Over and over again, she sucked on his lower lip, bit it, then kissed it better, and he couldn't bring himself to step back. So, there they remained, lost in each other until the elevator dinged announcing its arrival. At that point, they broke apart, both breathless.

"Come with me," she said hurriedly.

He looked askance. "It's unwise."

"Screw wise," she argued. She grabbed his hands and stepped into the elevator, pulling him with her.

Jon considered resisting but that would be denying himself of the only thing that made his world spin right now. Once inside, the doors closed and they were, effectively, alone. He pounced on her. He pushed her against the wall and grinned when her legs automatically wrapped themselves around his hips. Kissing her, he cupped her ass as she wriggled against him. He began to kiss her neck and moved a hand from her butt to grab a breast, the thin material of her dress no barrier at all as he felt her tight nipple against his palm. *No bra? Thin bra?* The thought was fleeting and he didn't give a damn; he was too busy savoring the woman who was as hungry as he.

VICTORIAN SURPRISE

The elevator slowed, and he didn't know if he was thankful they had arrived or annoyed that they'd have to stop. Either way, he pulled back from her and helped to make sure her dress was down as the doors opened. She grabbed his hand again and led the way to her room. As soon as they were on the other side of the door, she jumped him.

He scooped her up again as they resumed their voracious kissing. Holding her safely against him, he guided them toward the center of the room where he deposited her gently on the floor. There, he straightened back.

As much as he wanted to see this to the end, he worried that when the sun rose, she'd feel remorse for letting herself go. "I think it'd be wise for me to wish you a good night at this point."

She literally growled at him. "Screw wise," she repeated, then licked her lip. "Better yet, screw me." She seemed to consider what she was saying because a frown crossed her brow. "Or would you rather not?"

He scoffed. "I'd love nothing more than to take you until you can't remember your name, but I won't be the cause of regret come morning." Even if it meant permanent damage to his cock from pressing against the zipper of his trousers for so long.

"Is that the only reason? That I might regret being with you tonight?"

She ran a hand down the front of his shirt, her long, red nails scraping the cloth as she went. The look of it so erotic, he lost his train of thought for a moment. Eventually, he mumbled, "It's a rather heavy reason, don't you think?"

"What if…" Her words faltered. She licked her lips and tried again. "What if, just for tonight, I didn't want to think about the morning? What if tonight, I wanted to think only about you? About being with you." She gripped his lapels and held on. "Come on. Isn't that the whole point about coming to a place like this? It's an escape from reality. Not for forever, just for tonight." She tugged on his shirt as she stepped back. "Please, Jon. Just for tonight."

Her voice was so earnest, he didn't think he'd have the strength to walk away. It might be a mistake, but if she didn't want him to leave, he wouldn't; good morals be damned. "Just for tonight."

No Talking

There was no more talking for a while, only moans and gasps of pleasure. With no need to hold back, they returned to their ferocious kissing. Crazy with lust, she bit his shoulder through his shirt, but he didn't seem to mind. With a strong arm holding her tightly, Jon ran his lips along the line of her jaw, kissing and nibbling along the way. Sharon leaned back and moaned, giving him full access to her neck. Goosebumps burst through her body and her insides clenched in preparation for him. *Good God, he felt so good.*

Lost as she was in sensations, Sharon hadn't realized he had led them to the bed, but all of a sudden, he sat on the edge. The position put him right in front of her breasts. Growling, he pulled her between his legs and bit her nipple, ignoring the dress. Pleasure shot through her body and went straight to her core. Her weakened legs threatened to give out, so she held onto his shoulders, then ran her hands through his thick curls, holding him in place, wanting more.

Ignoring her wishes, he pulled back and tugged the loose top down. He pushed it until it landed just beneath her exposed chest, taking the flimsy lace of her bra with it and trapping her arms at her sides. Frustrated by her lack of mobility, she lost all thought when he worshiped her breasts with his mouth. He kissed them, sucked them, bit them gently, and then licked them better. From far away, she heard moans and realized they were her own.

It had been far too long since she'd been with a man and she couldn't wait to feel him, all of him, inside her. Pulling away from him, she shrugged the top back up so she could be free to touch him, then pushed him on his back to straddle him. Maybe she knew intuitively that they would end up like this because her choice of clothing for the night was perfect. The flowy material lay around them like an open flower, leaving her free to feel him between her legs.

Leaning forward to kiss him, she began to unbutton his shirt. It was annoyingly slow, so she ran her hands to the waist of his pants and tugged the material up, reveling in the tight abs she could feel beneath. Impatiently, she contemplated yanking until the buttons gave way, but decided to savor the moment instead. Leaning back, she felt his arousal at her core and undulated above him, giving them both so much pleasure, she thought she was about to shatter.

Jon had other ideas, though, because he wrapped his arms around her and sat up. Automatically, her arms went around his neck and her legs around his waist. Holding her safely against him, he flipped them and lay her on the bed beneath him. There, he lifted the dress to expose her lower body to his hungry gaze. Greedily, he looked at her, his stare as strong as a physical caress. His hand traced the same path as his eyes, and he stroked the skin of her rib cage, then lower to her hip. Hocking his fingers on either side of her panties, he pulled them until the thin lace was pushed over her knees, past her calves and feet, then tossed carelessly aside.

At the first touch, Sharon gasped and gripped the bedcovers tightly, her hands curled into fists. It was so light, just a finger running the length of her opening, top to bottom. Then, he did it again, this time with just a little more pressure. Her breathing became jagged and her heart threatened to leave her chest. At the third stroke, she couldn't bear it any more. "Please, Jon, please stop torturing me."

"Whatever your pleasure, love," he chuckled and pulled at her hips until she felt his mouth on her. She arched and cried out as his tongue slid over her clit. He kissed it, licked it, sucked at it, over and over again until she wanted to explode. Her body taut, the sensations washed over her. And when he filled her with his fingers, she arched as she climaxed, crying out in pleasure. Still, he didn't stop. Not until after every wave of bliss had run through her did she pull away from him, her sensitive body overwhelmed. Winded, she lay there and tried to catch her breath.

Jon went to lay beside her, looking at her with heavy eyes and a satisfied smile on his lips. That moment was possibly the most erotic one of her life. Never before had she felt so wanted, with pure, unabashed desire. Lusted. As he looked at her, full of hunger, she felt beautiful, sexy. And when he kissed her, she tasted herself on his tongue and loved it. It was a reminder of the ecstasy he'd just given her.

"Your turn," she told him. On weakened legs, Sharon stood in front of him and undid the rest of the buttons of his shirt as quickly as she could; which wasn't very fast considering her shaky hands. With each inch of his skin that was revealed, her desire grew anew and her insides began to clench again. She tugged his shirt and threw it aside, just as he had done with her panties. Pulling his hands to make him stand, his pants and boxers were next. He was the epitome of perfection: broad shoulders, lean hips, full erection. *Yum!*

When she would have crawled over him again, he shook his head and grabbed the bottom of her dress. Yanking it over her head, he let it fall at their feet. The bra soon followed.

After that, their need took over and they devoured each other. They kissed urgently, tongues coming together in an erotic dance, before moving to nibble necks, each taking turns. The pressure was strong enough to leave evidence on her neck, but she didn't care. She was enjoying every moment.

Splaying her hands on his chest, she let her fingers open wide before closing and tugging at the soft hair there.

He grabbed her breasts, pinching the nipples tightly.

With her nails, she scraped his skin before laying her palms flat against his tight nipples. She followed her touch with her mouth, kissing, then biting his nipples, then giving them a lick to soothe them.

His caress lowered to her hips and he pulled her closer so she could feel his hard erection against her core.

Sneaking her hands between them, she squeezed his rigid shaft, steel encased in silk. His sharp gasp followed by quick gulps of air were music to her ears.

She knew he'd had enough when he picked her up and dropped her on the bed. As soon as she landed, she spread her legs wide for him. He sheathed himself quickly with a condom before returning to her. Without wasting any time, he slammed into her. She closed her eyes and arched her back as her body stretched to accommodate his considerable size. He gave her barely a moment to breathe before his urgent need drove him into her, again and again, until her body shattered into a million pieces. Wave after wave of pleasure rippled through her. He wasn't done with her though, and each time he pounded into her again, echoes of sensations rippled, until his climax poured from his body. With a low, primitive growl of fulfillment, he collapsed on her.

Unable to move, they both lay there until they were able to catch their breath. It was a while before they recovered and the cold drove her under the blankets. Without a word, he joined her, and they dozed off, both lazy and sated.

The Morning

The morning came with an obnoxious ringing. Jon opened his eyes and remembered everything from the night before, including the woman whose warm, naked body he was spooning. Sleepily, she leaned forward and rolled her face on the pillow, tapping the nightstand repeatedly where the phone kept screeching, but never touching it.

"Good God, please stop..." Shae mumbled into the pillow, though she refused to get up and actually look for the phone. Uncaring about her plea, the phone continued. "For the love of all that is holy!"

Jon leaned up to rest his head on a fist, and with his free hand, brushed her hair from her nape. "You know, love," he said as he leaned in to kiss the exposed skin, "things are far easier when you open your eyes."

That seemed to wake her up. Suddenly, she rolled onto her back, eyes wide with shock, to look at him. "Jon," she breathed his name with surprise.

"Forget about me, did you?" He gave her an exaggerated frown. "I think I should be insulted that I'm so forgettable. I thought we had a brilliant time last night." Giving it another thought, he asked, "Or was that this morning?"

Ignoring his question, she reached for the phone and finally succeeded in grabbing it. When it finally quieted, she placed it on the bed beside her hip and looked at him.

VICTORIAN SURPRISE

Using the training that had become second nature, he read her body language. Needing to know how she felt about what had happened between them, he studied her for signs of remorse. Despite what she may have said yesterday, there was still a chance that she would regret what they'd done. Surprise was there, sure, in her wide eyes. He hoped it was because she expected him to leave during the night, and not something else. A slight frown passed over her features as she bit her lip, but she didn't say anything; she didn't jump out of bed and put distance between them, either. *That boded well, indeed.*

Instead, she scooted closer with a slight smile. As her tongue soothed her worried lip, her hand brushed his hair from his forehead. "Good morning," she said sweetly.

"Good morning," he echoed.

"You didn't leave," Shae confirmed his thoughts.

"Why would I leave the bed of the most beautiful woman on the planet?" The words were spoken without thought but were true, nevertheless. She was quite exquisite by the morning light, with a warm, relaxed smile on her full lips, eyes still dreamy with sleep, blonde strands scattered across her pillow.

Jon watched as her gaze turned playfully suspicious. With a sideways glint, she asked, "Are you looking to get laid again?"

"Maybe..." The word faded as he leaned in to kiss her. After a slow worship of her mouth, he asked, "Is there another, better way, to start the morning?"

"Well, honey," she said softly when he pulled away, "I prefer my mornings include a hot shower and some caffeine." She gave him a gentle tap on his chest before rolling to her side of the bed and jumping up. "Don't forget," she told him as she stood there, naked and comfortable in her own skin, "I have a wedding to attend."

With a sigh, he rolled onto his back and crossed his arms under his head. Laying there, he watched her turn and walk into the bathroom, appreciating the sexy sway of her hips, and her nice, round ass. The next time they were together, he was going to bite that ass. It was only fair, after all, considering how many times she had bit him. He'd lost count.

In the meantime, though, Alyssa would be waiting to meet him for breakfast, and Jon had to take his own shower.

Just as he was about to pull his pants on, Shae reappeared at the bathroom door and tilted her head. Still naked as a bird, she rested her hands on the door jambs. "Aren't you coming?" Looking at the trousers he still held, she said, "You weren't going to leave without saying goodbye, were you?" There was a wicked lift to her lips, one that left no doubt as to her thoughts.

Oh goodness, this woman was a delight! "Wouldn't dream of it." *Not when you look like that.*

Dropping his trousers to the floor, Jon joined her in a hot shower, made even hotter by the quick romp against the tiled wall. *Mental note to self, replace used condoms.* It had been a while since he'd had the pleasure of using both his backup and the backup to the backup. He snickered with satisfaction.

Afterwards, as they were drying each other off, he wondered when, or even *if*, he'd ever see her again. He wasn't ready to part ways just yet. Shae was a unique woman, relaxed and easy going, honest and expressive. He wanted more time to be with her.

But time wasn't on his side. Someone would be waiting for him and he had dallied longer than he should have already. He dressed quickly and then turned to watch her brush her hair as she stood by the sink. Beautiful in nothing but a robe, he appreciated the easy companionship he had with this woman he'd just met. Quietly, he said, "I hope you have a brilliant time at the wedding today. Yeah?"

Still running the brush through the silky tresses, she turned to face him and confirmed with an easy grin, "Yeah, of course."

Reluctant to leave, Jon went to her and, holding her face between his hands, he gave her one last passionate kiss before leaving. "Later then," he called as he left the bathroom.

Just as he was about to open the door to the hallway, he heard a knock from the other side. Jon froze. He had no desire to meet the brothers again, certainly not leaving their sister's room in the morning. Annoyed, he looked through the peephole, hoping for a hotel staff member. Not the brothers; it was Samantha, the fiancée. Without further hesitation, he opened the door and stepped out, only to find Sam—the brother—walking down the hall.

Their eyes met and Jon watched emotions play on Sam's face. Furious, his hands curled into fists and he strode down the corridor ready for a fight. "Good morning, lovebirds," Jon said cheerfully, hoping that Sam would calm down and see reason. "It's a lovely day for a wedding, isn't it?" He wouldn't start a brawl on his wedding day, would he?

Without a word, Sam swung for Jon's head. *Damn it.*

"Honey!" Samantha called out.

Jon ducked easily and raised his hands before him in a passive gesture, palms out. Though it looked innocent enough, it was also an active defensive pose to parry any swing attempts. "Oy, come now, mate," Jon tried again, "you don't want to do this." Another swing from Sam, but Jon leaned back, easily avoiding it and slapped Sam's fist with an open hand.

"Sammy, stop it!" Samantha tried again.

Hearing the noise, Sharon came out of the room still dressed in a robe, hair wet. In his peripheral vision, Jon saw her looking at them and shake her head. "Are you two kidding me right now?" she asked, annoyance clear in her tone. Unafraid, she placed herself between them, her back to Jon while she faced her brother. Putting both hands on his chest, she said nonchalantly, "He's an MMA fighter. Are you sure you want to do this?"

"For fuck's sake, Shae!" Sam hissed. "You just met him."

Jon relaxed his stance and watched as she pushed him several steps down the corridor. She spoke to him softly enough that only Sam could hear, and Jon watched Sam's expression turn from furious to just irritated. Still listening, Sam ran an angry hand through his hair. "Fine," Sam declared when she finished. Jon knew things weren't really fine, but for now, he'd let it go.

Sharon turned to Samantha and said, "Good morning, Sam! Come in, honey. You're going to look positively radiant today!" Ignoring the men, she closed the door on them.

Jon looked at Sam and waited for his reaction first. If he was going to start swinging again, then Jon would act accordingly. But without a word, Sam turned and walked back the way he came.

"All right, then..." Jon muttered to himself. Maybe it was for the best that he wouldn't be seeing Sharon

VICTORIAN SURPRISE

again. He didn't think the rest of the family would welcome him with open arms.

With a last look at the closed door, Jon left to meet up with Alyssa.

A Wedding?

The chapel Samantha had selected was warm and welcoming, decorated with large, lush plants. The waterfall fountain in the corner made soothing sounds and gave the interior an outdoorsy feel that wouldn't be possible if they were really outside, certainly not on the Vegas strip. The room was large enough to comfortably seat a small number of family and friends, if any had joined them. But there were only six individuals present that morning: the bride and groom; along with Sharon as the maid of honor; Scott as the best man; Sarah filled in as a bridesmaid, or matron since she was married; and lastly, the minister performing the ceremony.

Some would be unhappy with such a setup, but as Sharon looked at Samantha and Sammy, she saw utter bliss. These two didn't need much; just each other.

Before the ceremony had started, one of the chapel's staff members had offered her tissues, which she had promptly rejected. Sharon wasn't one of those sappy women who cried at the drop of a hat. But now, she wished she hadn't. Her eyes filled and threatened to ruin her hour-long makeup application.

Looking at Sammy, about to marry an amazing woman who loved him for who he was—flaws and all—Sharon was thankful that Samantha had barged her way into his life the way she had. There was a time, before Sharon had pushed him to take Samantha in, that Sharon feared Sammy might end up alone. But now, there they stood, side by side; he, looking

VICTORIAN SURPRISE

handsome in his tuxedo; and she, looking stunningly gorgeous in a shimmering, white gown that rippled at her waist. The A-symmetrical cut of the skirt ended just above the knees in the front and flowed longer by the sides and back, making her legs look even longer.

Blinking back the tears, Sharon focused on Sammy, who was speaking his vows, and she couldn't help but laugh as she listened to his words.

"I promise not to kill you and leave your body to the wolves. I promise not to throw your phone out the window when I get tired of listening to your horrible music. I promise to listen to every word you ramble, even when my eyes glaze over and I want to stab myself."

The minister's eyes grew round and he frowned as his gaze bounced between the two people before him. To his credit, he didn't say anything.

"I promise to make you your favorite breakfast on your birthday, every year, and share my bacon every day." Sammy continued, "I promise to love you every day of my life, even when you're being the biggest pain in the ass. I love you, Samantha Waters."

"Oh, Sammy," Samantha said, her voice cracking. She took a deep breath and began, "I promise to trust you and not question when you're driving me to some random place in the middle of nowhere. I promise to keep my ramblings down to a minimum, so you don't have to stab yourself." At that, she rolled her eyes. "Well, I promise to *try*, anyway."

Sharon saw Sammy's raised eyebrow as Samantha shrugged.

"I promise to occasionally play music you enjoy. I promise to take my epinephrine pen everywhere I go.

And I promise to love you for the rest of your life, and every day of mine."

When the silence stretched and it seemed Samantha had nothing else to say, the minister was about to speak, but Sammy leaned over to Samantha and whispered, "You forgot 'obey.'"

Shaking her head, she replied in the same tone, "No, I didn't."

A low growl emanated from him.

Samantha smiled and countered, "Remember, you already promised not to kill me."

"No," he challenged, "I promised not to kill you and leave your body to the wolves. I didn't say anything about the bears."

Laughing, Samantha hit him with her bouquet. Petals flew.

When they had both settled, they looked to the confused minister. He frowned at them and asked, "Um… Do you want to continue?"

Samantha quickly answered, "Of course," while Sammy gave him a *duh* look.

"Okay," the minister said, perplexed. "You may now exchange the rings."

Sammy went first and put the ring on Samantha's finger. Sharon laughed when he snickered and stopped halfway. With an exaggerated sigh, Samantha shook her head and pushed her hand forward until the ring was fully on. There was no hesitation when she placed his ring on. If anything, it was done rather quickly and efficiently.

Instead of making the usual declaration, the minister's voice rose with the question, "I now pronounce you husband and wife…?"

VICTORIAN SURPRISE

As soon as the last word was out, Samantha threw her bouquet carelessly over her shoulder and jumped onto Sammy, wrapping her arms around his neck and her legs around his waist. He held her tightly and, oblivious to their surroundings, they kissed passionately.

Still baffled, the minister asked, "You may now kiss?"

Looking to put the poor man at ease, Sharon leaned to him and said, "That's normal for them. And they're very happy." Laughing, she bent down to pick up the beaten bouquet off the floor. Across from her, Scott was telling the newlyweds to get a room.

Sammy eventually put Samantha down, and holding hands, they led the way out.

Al's Girlfriend

"Why the rush to Vegas, Al?" Jon asked Alyssa.

They were sitting in a local restaurant waiting for their food, having been seated after exchanging a quick hug. It had been a long time since they had seen each other.

In the years they had been apart, her dark hair had been cut short into a style that curled around her face. It looked cute on her. But her once smooth face had aged far quicker than it should have, showing lines that hadn't been there before. Her bright brown eyes had dulled, and there was a tightness around her lips. She had also lost weight, too much. He didn't need detective training to know that she'd been hiding things from him. Texts can only do so much when individuals were thousands of miles apart.

Instead of answering the question, Al laughed. "You sound so weird with that accent."

Going with the flow, he joked with her, "I'll have you know, the ladies love it."

Snickering, she slapped his arm. "That's because they don't know you like I do."

"And you're going to keep that information to yourself, yeah? Yeah." He joked, "Don't forget, I have some serious blackmail info on you."

Alyssa had been Jon's best friend since they had been high school sweethearts. It hadn't taken them long to realize that something wasn't quite right with their relationship. While their friends were hitting home runs in the bedroom, Al had no interest in anything beyond kissing. And even then, he had always been the one to kiss her, and she'd let him.

Two months into their relationship, Jon had caught Al staring at his friend's *girlfriend* at a party, and once they were alone, he'd called her out on it. She had denied it, and he had let it go, but he always kept an eye on her.

"Yeah, you do." Al smiled. In a more somber tone, she added, "I've missed you."

"I've missed you, too, Al." He took a sip of his drink before he asked, "How's Emily?"

Quickly, Alyssa said, "Oh, good." Locking eyes with him and nodding, she continued, "Fine. Oh, better than fine. She's great." She gave him a bright smile.

Automatically, his internal lie detector flashed: a fake smile that didn't reach her eyes; fidgeting in her seat; fixing and adjusting the silverware in front of her repeatedly; making too long eye contact when she wasn't avoiding his gaze altogether.

"Why are you lying? You know I can tell when you're lying to me, Al." He wouldn't have pressed the issue, but he knew her. If he didn't broach it, she wouldn't have said a word. "How's Emily?" Jon repeated. As she opened her mouth to speak, he interrupted, "And don't you dare say 'everything's fine' when I know it isn't."

Resigned, Alyssa said, "Emily is... um..." She faltered as her voice cracked. Shaking her head, she leaned back and crossed her arms. "She's got something bad and um... she's refusing to talk to me... and no one is telling me anything..." She turned and looked out of the window. When she turned back, she continued sharply. "I need her in my life, Jon, every day from now until—" Abruptly, she stopped.

Jon waited for more, but it didn't come. "Something bad? That's all you're going to give me? I've known you since we were kids. I know you better than your parents know you." He reached out and grabbed both her hands. Squeezing them gently, he pushed, "You should have told me, Al. You called me, asked me to throw a wedding together in a big hurry with no additional information, and I did it without question. But I'm asking now."

She shook her head and blinked back the tears. "Don't. Don't make me say it." She tried to pull her hands back, but he wouldn't let her go. "Just don't."

The years between them faded away and Jon saw her as she once was, a scared teenager, afraid of being exposed, of being vulnerable. He had been gentle with her then, had given her space. Eventually, she had come to him and confessed, not that he hadn't figured it out on his own. At that point, anyone who knew her, really knew her, knew the truth. Since then, they'd been best mates.

He had understood her need to hide. That tidbit of information would not have gone over well in her home. Her parents would have freaked out, beaten her, and then sent her somewhere to be *fixed*. So for the next couple of years, they had acted the impeccable couple, until she went off to college. After that, there were no more relationship conversations. Using the excuse that she wanted to further her career, and didn't want to be held back by a husband and some kids, she excelled. Becoming the successful president of a marketing company had kept her parents at bay.

VICTORIAN SURPRISE

But hiding for so long had taken its toll. Especially during the holidays, when she'd had to visit family and was forced to leave her girlfriend behind.

And just like all those years ago, Alyssa was going to need time to get acclimated to the situation, whatever it was. Coercing her to share what she clearly wasn't ready to, wouldn't be doing her any favors. What she needed right now was unconditional love and support. That's what Jon would give her.

"Okay, Al," Jon said softly, giving her hands another squeeze. "I'm here. And I'll stand by you tomorrow, and I'll be there with you when the time comes..." He let the rest go unspoken, knowing she understood.

Jon pulled back when the food arrived, and Al thanked the waiter but never looked up. In the pretense of grabbing some salt, she turned to the side to hide the tears and didn't look back until he was gone. Facing back to Jon, she said, "Make me cry in public again, and I'll tell your next girlfriend you wet the bed after your graduation party."

"I did not!" he denied vehemently. "That was spilled beer and you know it."

"No, Jason and I both agreed. It smelled like pee."

Just like that, the moment had passed and he fully expected the rest of their meal to be spent with good memories and some laughs.

For a fleeting second, Jon wondered how Shae would react if she heard Al say that he had wet the bed. Though he doubted Shae would believe her, she would probably look at him and laugh. Women tended to stick together. "I forgot to mention. My friend, Shae, wishes you and Emily many happy years together."

Alyssa looked up with a raised eyebrow. "Who's Shae?"

Lena Lane

Jon wondered how to describe her and chose truthfully simple. "She's someone I met on the flight here. Her brother's getting married this morning. Although, by now, the wedding is probably over."

"Will you see her again?" The question was full of the complications women were known for.

Men were much simpler. "Doubtful."

Lunch Drama

The five of them were waiting for their lunch table when Sarah approached Sharon and asked, "Why are you grinning like the cat who swallowed the canary?"

Sharon gave her a sideways glance. "What're you talking about?" she asked, feigning ignorance.

"Spill it," Sarah demanded with a laugh, her warm, brown eyes bright with the expectation of some juicy gossip.

"Sarah, honey," Sharon insisted, eyes wide with contrived innocence, "there's nothing to 'spill.'" She shrugged and shook her head. Unable to control her telltale smile, she bit her lips into submission.

"Liar!" Sarah challenged, grinning. "You look like the Cheshire cat." In a quick move, she planted herself in front of Sharon, looking at her straight on. "This has something to do with the guy from the plane, doesn't it?"

The hostess came to guide them to their table, giving Sharon a small reprieve. Sam and Sam followed her, lost in each other as they were, but Sarah kept her position and blocked Sharon's path. Scott took only a few steps before turning to look for his wife. Sharon had to give Sarah something or all four of them would be on her, with questions she had no intention of answering. Even now, Scott was eyeing her with a curious gleam, head tilted slightly, while he watched them.

In spite of what the Sams had seen that morning, Sharon was fairly certain neither of them told Scott and

Sarah anything; Sammy didn't speak unless pushed, and Samantha only blurted stuff out when nervous. So Sharon went with a partial truth. "Listen, honey, I'm just happy that both of my brothers are so in love with their wives." She gave Sarah a dazzling smile and wrapped her arm around her shoulders. Spinning her, she gently nudged Sarah forward. "Come on."

On the way, Sarah whispered, "I don't believe you, but I'm happy that you're happy."

Sharon smiled to herself, but didn't reply. Her persona may be outgoing, but she liked to keep her private life private. And though she may love both her brothers and new sisters dearly, her sex life was not something she was going to share with them.

At least, that's what she thought. Halfway through lunch, during a quiet moment, Scott turned to her and said, "You can't see him anymore." All of a sudden, the whole table was looking at her.

Frowning, Sharon looked up. "What?" she asked, her fork halfway to her mouth. "Who are you talking about?"

Surprisingly, Sammy was the one to clarify. "The guy from the plane."

Sharon looked at him, shocked. "Excuse me?" Adrenaline began to pump through her veins, her heart pounded in her chest, and her stomach tightened with nerves. *They couldn't be serious.* Since when did any of them have a right to tell her who she could or couldn't see?

"I'm not gonna just sit around and watch some asshole pork my little sister." Sammy, the quiet one who usually stayed out of everyone's business, growled out. He was leaning back in his chair, watching her with a stone face and icy eyes.

VICTORIAN SURPRISE

Since when did Sammy give a damn about her relationships? Her belly churned with anger, and she took a deep, soothing breath. This was his wedding day and she didn't want to fight with him. It was supposed to be a happy time.

Whether or not she chose to see Jon again was none of their business. Even *she* didn't know if she'd see him again. As far as she was concerned, what happened that morning was an oddity, born from feeling free for the first time in years.

The bigger issue was their belief that they could bully her into an outdated view of what was proper behavior for a woman. *They couldn't be serious*, her mind echoed. Just to confirm she wasn't reading them wrong, she brushed her hair back with a shaking hand and asked, "Why is that?"

It was Scott who answered. "Because you don't know anything about him." Unlike Sam, he leaned forward, closer to Sharon, and spoke softly. "He's not American, and you know he's not going to hang around for you. He's just going to use you and then go back where he came from." He straightened back in his chair. "Besides, his name is John, right? He doesn't even have an S name. He doesn't fit with us." Nonchalantly, he took a bite of his food.

As Sharon's fury grew, her breathing became ragged. "You fucking asshole," she hissed through clenched teeth. "How fucking dare you; you don't know a damn thing about him." Her eyes flashed from one brother to the other. "Hypocrites!" Forcing her voice to stay as low and even as possible, she clenched her hands into fists by her plate. Looking at Scott, she said, "You have no right to judge me after what you and Sarah did at the colonial property." She tried to ignore the sharp gasp from Sarah's direction, but said, "I was the one who changed the sheets." Turning to Sammy, Sharon reminded him sharply, "And I know all about your unholy trinity."

"Wow, Shae," Sammy said, his voice gravelly. "You sound pissed."

"Of course I'm pissed." She didn't bother to look up. With a shaky hand, she grabbed her fork. "I'm furious."

"Karma." Sammy snickered. "I hear she's a bitch, right?"

What the hell? Was that laughter she heard in his tone? Sharon looked up and saw a mischievous look in his eyes, one she hadn't seen in a long while. Not since before their mother died.

Scott was the next to speak. "Do you remember the ice cube incident on the fourth of July?"

Sharon closed her eyes and passed a hand over her face, all energy fading from her, leaving her empty. She was going to kill them, kill them both, if this was a prank.

"Yeah," Sammy said, voice infused with laughter, even if he didn't laugh out loud, "remember how *helpful* you were with Samantha?"

"I'm not sure 'helpful' is the appropriate term, Sammy," Scott said, his voice also hinting at his amusement. "Wouldn't you say 'meddling' is more appropriate?"

Sharon looked up in time to see both girls holding back their laughter. "It's not funny." She pointed her fork at them threateningly and tried to look fierce, but her relief overpowered her anger. Her breathing still ragged, she joked, "I'm going to kill you." She looked at the four of them and saw the humor in their eyes. "All of you." She shook her head. "I thought you were serious, damn it. I think I even got a gray hair because of it." Pulling her hair forward, she began to look for it.

"Well, now you know what it feels like," Scott said, unmercifully, "when other people stick their noses into your business. Now," grabbing some more food, he asked, "what's this about an unholy trinity?"

"Never mind," Sammy quickly interjected, the humor gone. "Tell us about him, Shae," he demanded as he took a drink from his soda, "because, if he hurts you, we *will* kill him."

The Spy

Jon watched them have lunch and tried not to stare. It hadn't been his intention to spy on them. He'd been on his way to his room and decided to get a quick drink before heading up. Moments after making himself comfortable at the bar, he saw the hostess seat them. Completely unexpected. He decided that he'd finish his drink and leave, but Shae kept pulling his gaze. Just like at the airport, Jon couldn't drag his eyes away from her graceful elegance. He'd bet she was an excellent dancer.

Evidently, none of them had any experience with dangerous situations. All five of them were oblivious to his presence even though he watched them the entire time. If he'd had ulterior motives and any of them had been his mark, they'd be screwed. He couldn't understand it. Even before he entered adulthood, he was acutely aware of everyone around him. He'd learned at quite a young age how significant that lesson was.

Not that he *wanted* them to know. The only motive he had for his continued interest was the gorgeous blonde whose curves filled her dress to perfection. Once again, her pale, silky hair was loose around her bare shoulders. Absently, she brushed it back off her face, tucking it behind her ear and giving him an ideal view of her profile.

Jon had considered leaving after his first drink, but during their walk to the table, there had been some discussion that Shae wanted no part of. She dismissed the girl easily enough, but the same subject had reoccurred, or another just as distressing. Even from his position at the bar, he could see how tense her body had become. Oh, she was riled, all right, furious even. At one point, her hands were curled into fists by her plate. But when he looked at the others, he saw no evidence of anger, just amusement. Jon had almost gone to her then, with the intention of putting a stop to whatever they were discussing. The four of them were having fun at her expense, and he didn't like it one bit. If they didn't stop it immediately, he would.

Just as he stood to take action, she ran a hand over her face with a barely perceptible shake of her head and he saw her body visibly relax. *What happened?* Her straight back loosened up and she almost slouched. While holding her head in a hand, she had turned to him with her eyes closed and he could see her smile. Whatever the issue was, it had been resolved. He, too, relaxed and sat back down.

Things had calmed, but instead of leaving, he remained. *You're acting like a total creep. You have no reason to keep watching them.*

It was true, but they were such an oddity. To him, anyway. They weren't a family of drunken idiots who went around destroying everything they had in an intoxicated stupor. They didn't beat each other up; though Jon imagined Sam could, and would, destroy anyone if those he cared about were in danger. *He'd try, anyway.* He'd already proven the point that morning. Hell, they all worked together. Who in their right mind would work with family? It was such a horrid idea.

Also, what had they been discussing that caused Shae such distress? She may be smiling and laughing now, but not too long ago, she'd been so enraged, her tiny hand had grabbed a fork like a weapon. Would she feel the need to fight again?

Would she even know how? Jon doubted she knew how to throw a punch to save her life. No, her only defense was her charm and wit. It may work in some situations but not all. He knew first-hand how ugly some situations could get. His imagination turned dark and he saw her in one of his files, a lifeless victim in a picture, her eyes open but vacant.

Shaking the image away, he returned his attention to the table and evaluated the five of them. More often than not, her brothers ignored her. The other two women were sweet and useless.

Perhaps he should send them all invitations to self-defense classes as soon as his dojo was up and running. In the meantime, he had to do everything he could to keep her safe, because that vision of her unseeing eyes would give him nightmares like he hadn't experienced since he was a kid living at home.

Plus One

Busy?

The simple text came through as Sharon was working after dinner. Seeing Jon's number made her stomach drop in delicious excitement. She had thought about texting him all day but didn't know if he was with his friend. Instead, she had filled her time with lunch, work, some more work, some dinner, and back to work.

No. Send. If she had told him the truth, he would probably stop texting and she really didn't want that. Besides, she was down to ten emails. There would be plenty of time to deal with them when she was back at the office. She ignored the hysterical laughter that tried to escape her at that though. Who was she kidding? She'd be back to work as soon as their conversation ended.

How was the wedding? he asked.

Sharon closed the laptop for the time being, and curled into bed before replying. *It was what anyone would expect from them. He promised not to kill her. She promised not to talk him to death.* Send.

His reply was quick. *How romantic? I think?*

LOL That's what the minister thought, too. Send. *But they're happy and that's all that matters.* Send.

Good. A moment later, *Did you catch the bouquet?*

If by 'catch' you mean 'pick up off' the floor, then yes. Send.

Lucky you. As she was thinking of something to say, another text came through. *I never asked if you had someone at home, waiting impatiently for your return.*

No. Of course not. Send. If she had, she never would have slept with him. What was he thinking? Then a more pressing thought passed through her mind: did he? She had to know. *You?* Send.

No, of course not, he echoed. Then, *When do you go back?*

Redeye, day after tomorrow. Send. *Five days away from the office is long enough to cause chaos.* Send.

Jon's reply to that statement was slower coming through. *Safe travels to you and your family.*

If only. But no; this trip was a solo one. *Thank you but I'm the only one returning home.* Send. *Scott and Sarah are headed to Fiji and the two Sams are staying for a full week.* Send. *I'm sure my trip will be quite safe, though. I'm using the same airline for the return trip and I've heard they have a clean record. No crashes. At all.* Send.

A one-word retort from him, *Funny.*

What about you? When do you head home? Send.

Sharon lay on her bed looking at her phone as she waited for his answer. Seconds became minutes and still, no reply came. Was that the end of their conversation?

She had known this connection with him would end when reality returned. As she had said last night—or was that this morning?—this trip was an escape from her mundane day to day existence back home. She had wanted nothing more than just a momentary break, a passing fling with him. And, boy, did he deliver.

Perhaps she should be ashamed of herself for using him as she had, but he'd been there, available and willing, or willing after some encouraging words. Gentleman that he was, he would have left her, but she was oh so glad he hadn't.

Finally, the phone dinged again. *I'll also be on the redeye. Wow, that's a coincidence.* Send.

VICTORIAN SURPRISE

Again, the minutes passed and no reply. Eventually, he said, *I don't want you on a plane alone.*

With a frown, she wondered what he meant by that. Had he changed his flight just so he could accompany her? Because that's what it sounded like. What was he thinking? That she was some damsel in distress? Unable to take care of herself? Ire growing with each thought, she replied, *Sweet, but I've been on my own for several years now.* Send. *Believe it or not, I'm perfectly capable of traveling alone.* Send.

His next text defused her growing anger. *I know you're capable. But I'd love to stare into your beautiful eyes while you hold my hands one last time. Before we go our separate ways.*

Damn, he was good. *Have I told you how charming you are?* Send.

Yes, but I never tire of hearing it. Please continue.

Grinning, she trapped her lower lip between her teeth. *Charming, handsome, amazing.* Send. *Skilled.* Send. *Delicious.* Send. *Tantalizing.* Send. *And so very big...* Send.

How I love the way you think.

If she continued on this path, she was going to call him over for a repeat of their morning together. Though she'd love it, she hadn't slept much last night and she had a lot of work to do. Maybe she should change the subject. Grudgingly, she sent: *LOL How did the meeting with your friend go?* Responsibilities really sucked ass.

Not as well as I'd hoped. Immediately after, *Her fiancée is dying and they want to marry before that happens. It's a rather sad love story.*

Well, shit. *That's so heartbreaking. I'm so sorry.* Send. *Is there anything I can do?*

A couple of minutes went by before the response came through. *Care to be my plus one?*

Sharon frowned at her phone. Wouldn't it be a little weird? They'd just met. She told him as much. *Wouldn't it be strange? Taking someone you've just met to a wedding?*

Nah. Only her friends and their main squeeze are attending. Aly's family doesn't know. Her work mates don't know. Emily and I are the only two that she opens up to. A second later, *She's annoyingly secretive.*

Wait, are you telling me that you're the only guest on Aly's side? Send.

Technically, I'm her best man. Emily's family and friends have adopted her, though. Everyone there will be there to support both of them. But your company would be lovely.

Sharon tried to imagine living a lie for all of her adult life, hiding who she was from everyone around her, never having support during a breakup. She couldn't. It was as bad as Samantha's story and having no family. Thinking about it, she imagined it to be worse. Wouldn't it be better to have no one at all than to be surrounded by people you couldn't talk to?

Okay. Send.

Brilliant. We'll chat more in the morning. G'night.

Horrible Movie

It was almost midnight and she was still looking at potential properties for her newest client when the text came through. *Are you still up?*

Sharon was surprised to Jon's text. She thought they were be done chatting for the evening, especially since they'd already said their goodnights. Still, she answered honestly, *Yes. What's up?*

Will you do me a favor?

Interesting. Frowning with curiosity, she sent, *Depends. What kind?*

Will you touch yourself for me?

Her heart thumped in her chest. Was he asking her to do what she thought he was? *What?* Send. Quickly after, *Where?* Send.

Your breast. The right one. After a second, another came through, *Pinch the nipple hard for me.*

Sharon sat there, staring at the phone like it was a foreign object. She forgot that the little tool she held could be used for good things, *fun* things. How long had it been since she'd had anything close to phone sex? Jon was making this trip to Vegas far more pleasant that she could ever have imagined. Putting her laptop away, for the night this time, she followed his instructions, her breath growing heavy, the pressure between her legs mounting. *I did.* Send.

Do the same to the other now.

Without hesitation, she did as she was told. *I did it.* Send.

Good. Now, put the phone down and do it to both at the same time. Make sure you squeeze them hard. Pinch the nipples until they ache. Tell me when you're done.

She did it. She clasped the mounds tightly, and when she pinched her nipples, she felt the sensation all the way to her core. Her insides throbbed and she wanted him there. *Done.*

Good. What I need you to do now is to take your hand and slide it under your panties. Then, I want you to part your lips and stroke your clit with your finger. When you're wet and aching, I want you to slide your fingers inside. Will you do that for me? Will you do that over and over again until you come for me?

Oh good God, he wanted her to explode. *No!* Send. *I want YOU to do it.* Send.

Even though she told him no, she did it. Step by step, she did as he asked. She touched and caressed her own body over and over again. And when her insides clenched and she needed him there, to fill her, she slid her fingers inside and pretended they were him. With the heel of her palm, she rubbed her clit as her fingers went as deep as they could. The pressure built and her body grew taut, and just as she was about to shatter, there was a knock at her door.

Angrily, she growled incoherently. They could just go play in traffic!

Another stroke; she was so close. Her body begged her not to stop, but when she heard Jon call her name from the hallway, her eyes flew open and she rushed to let him in.

The door hadn't fully closed behind him before they started. They kissed and struggled to remove their clothing as they stumbled towards the bed. Naked, she climbed onto the bed on hands and knees and when she would have flipped over, he stopped her. Sliding a

VICTORIAN SURPRISE

couple of fingers into her wet warmth, he leaned forward and nipped hard on a luscious ass cheek. She would have laughed at the sting if she wasn't so focused on the pleasure of being so full. With heavy lids, she looked back at him and saw the corner of an empty condom wrapper trapped in his teeth. He pulled away just long enough to cover himself. And when he slid into her, she cried out and shattered.

Her body shuddered around him as she convulsed in orgasm. But Jon was just getting started. Over and over, he slammed into her, sending ripples of her climax through her, again and again. She was astonished. Even though waves of pleasure from her first orgasm still rippled through her, her body was getting ready to come again. The sweet pressure was building. On her hands and knees, she grabbed a pillow and gripped it tightly, her hands curling into fists on the edges. Suddenly, Jon plunged deeply and growled, throbbing within her as he spilled himself, triggering paroxysm of orgasmic pleasure through Sharon's entire being as she exploded around him.

Spent and sated, they collapsed on the bed; she was face forward on the pillow and slack; he lay on his back beside her. Gasping for breath and waiting for their hearts to return to normal, they looked at each other.

"Thank you," she murmured breathlessly, "for coming to my assistance. Your..." she paused to consider the right word, "equipment is very useful."

"Have I been reduced to being your toy?" he joked, breathless himself.

She chuckled. "Are you against being used as walking dildo?"

"I think I might be, yeah." Luckily for her, there was no offense in his tone.

Lena Lane

Sharon remembered the flight and how he had helped her through it, how he'd encouraged her to pursue her dream, how sweetly he talked about love. There was a lot more to this man than just great sex, but she was too drained to talk about it at the moment.

Unexpectedly, Jon sat up and leaned on his elbows. "I'm famished. Have you had dinner?"

Hugging her pillow, she told him, "I have, yes." She watched as disappointment filled his eyes. "Delivery?"

With a grin, he jumped of the bed and called out for delivery. While they waited for his food, they snuggled together under the sheets, and Sharon started flipping through the channels. All of a sudden, he blurted out, "Oy, stop there!" It was a commercial for body wash. Quickly, he said, "No, go back one." She did. "Yeah, here. Brilliant movie, yeah. And perfect timing, it's just starting."

She arched her brow at him. What he was calling a great movie was a horrible B movie, probably from the sixties, complete with terrible acting and worse special effects. Sharon scoffed. "Uh, no," and changed the channel.

"Aw, come now, love," Jon said, with wide eyes and a flashing grin. "It's a classic."

"Yeah," she replied sarcastically. "A classic that should have stayed in nineteen-sixty." She continued looking for something better while he tried to change her mind.

"It's from the fifties, thank you. And it's got superb actors from the time."

"How about we watch something that won't rot our brains?" She found a show on remodeling. Arching an inquisitive brow at him, she waited for his answer.

VICTORIAN SURPRISE

"No, no, no," Jon said quickly. "You are not forcing your job on me."

Laughing, she countered, "My job does not involve remodeling. It involves staging, thank you very much. Besides," she scooted up and the sheet fell down to her waist, baring her breasts to his hungry eyes, "it's always smart to learn new things from others."

"Shae, love," he turned to her and caressed her cheek with the back of his fingers. "First, you will not distract me with your very delectable breasts." His head bobbled a little bit in thought. With the corner of his lip raised and laughter in his eyes, he mused, "Though if you give me a half hour, it may work.

"Second," his dark eyes focused on her and continued, "you work enough. Relax for a change, yeah?"

"But—"

"No buts, Shae." He settled himself back down onto the pillows and pulled her with him. "Don't think I didn't notice the laptop sitting on the nightstand. Admit it, you were working when I texted, weren't you?"

"Fine," she said and changed the channel back to the horrible B movie, "but I'm going to talk through the whole thing."

That turned out to be all right because he talked through the whole thing, too. When the food came, he quickly put his boxers on and went to the door. He brought the food back to bed and they spent the next couple of hours laughing at the screen while she ate his fries. She hadn't intended to eat any, but he offered. And when she was done with one, Jon gave her another, and then another. The next thing she knew, the food was gone, the movie was finished, and they were snuggled together.

Lena Lane

Though she knew he would be leaving soon, she wasn't ready to get him go. With lazy moves, she drew circles on his chest and played connect-the-dots with the freckles scattered on his skin. "Stay the night?" Sharon whispered hopefully.

Somberly, Jon brushed her hair from her face and tucked it behind her ear. His dark eyes were unfathomable and she wondered what he was thinking. A stray lock of hair fell onto his forehead as he leaned down to her and whispered, "Whatever your pleasure, love." He gave her a gentle kiss.

Cheat Day

"Shut it, bastard…" Shae mumbled into her pillow.

Jon wasn't sure if the profanity was directed at him or the phone that kept ringing, but he hoped it was the latter considering he hadn't spoken. His eyes still heavy with sleep, he watched as she slapped randomly on the nightstand looking for the phone, never connecting. Deja vu.

"For the love of all that is holy!" Sharon pushed herself up far enough to see where the phone was and slapped at it, several times. Eventually, she hit the right spot, because the obnoxious sound finally stopped. With a sigh of appreciation at the silence, she let go and flopped back down, face first.

Shae is not a fan of mornings, Jon observed with a snicker. He wondered if she knew he was still there. Doubtful. If she had, she would have commented. Instead, she wrapped her arms around the pillow and snuggled deeper into it.

What had she said yesterday? She liked to begin her day with a coffee and a shower? Maybe he'd make her day by getting her a freshly brewed cup. He could certainly use one. But Jon wasn't sure if he could get dressed and leave without waking her. Still, he was awake and was restless to get his day started.

Attempting to make as little noise as possible, he got up and dressed. On his way to the door, he swiped the room key off the dresser, then left. Her rhythmic breathing never wavered.

Lena Lane

Jon was only gone for about a half hour, but he still expected her to be awake by the time he returned. He was wrong. Shae was in the same position he'd left her in, still breathing deeply. Jon wondered if she realized how exhausted she was. Working all day and night wasn't healthy, and he was going to make sure she had at least one cheat day while she was here. He would make it his mission.

Assuming, of course, that she didn't have plans.

And if she did, he'd just have to convince her that *his* plan was better.

Brilliant.

Lethal Dancer

The smell of coffee teased her, as did the aroma of fresh bread. They both beckoned to Sharon like breakfast sirens, pulling her from the warm embrace of her bed, one she was reluctant to leave. Torn between sleeping her day away and feeding her grumbling tummy, the lure of delicious food won out.

Barely awake, she expected to hear one of her brothers in the kitchen, demanding she wake up for some reason or another, complaining that they were already late for some meeting. But when she finally opened her eyes, she was shocked to see Jon, wearing nothing but his boxers, doing some sort of exercise drill in her hotel room. Walking from the window to the door, he was punching and kicking some invisible foe, occasionally ducking and swaying. Sharon assumed that was to avoid getting hit by the nonexistent opponent, but she wasn't sure.

What she did know was that the sexiest man on the planet was in her room right now. His lithe muscles flexed beneath his skin as he moved, his punches were lightning fast, and his lethal kicks were as beautiful to watch as a dancer. Never before had she wanted anyone as much as she wanted this man. In her bed. Now.

Yet she didn't want him to stop. Ever.

Jon hadn't been lying when he told her he was an MMA fighter. Though difficult to reconcile the kick-ass warrior she was watching with the romantic she was spending time with, there was no doubt he had amazing skill. He was exquisite. Wanting to get a better view, she sat up.

Unfortunately for her, he stopped as soon as he noticed she was awake.

"Good morning, love," Jon grinned and swept his hand over his face, wiping away the glistening droplets of sweat.

One of them rolled down the middle of his chest, and she wanted to run her nail over the trail, follow it down to his belly button, and then past it. *Oh good God!* If anyone ever knew that she'd come to find sweat on a man sexy, she'd die. But then she thought about it. She couldn't be the only one, could she?

Tucking her hair behind her ear, Sharon said, "Please don't stop on my account." She hoped she didn't sound desperate, but she wanted more. Lots more.

"Nah, I was just keeping myself busy." He went into the bathroom for a towel and stood in the doorway while using it. "Sorry for the look, but I don't have any other clothes with me."

At that, she laughed. "Please don't apologize. This is… ah… quite a sight to wake up to."

A worried frown crossed his face. "Not scary I hope?"

"No, no, no," Sharon quickly denied. "Quite the opposite, actually." She got up from bed and did exactly as she'd fantasized moments before. She ran a long fingernail down the trail of the droplet, down his chest, past his belly button. And though she was tempted to go inside his boxers, her stomach growled loudly. *Damn it! Talk about a mood killer.*

"Oh, Shae," he said in a husky whisper, "how I love the way you think." He pulled away to throw the towel onto the bathroom floor. "But I do believe breakfast is a priority. Besides, we'll have plenty of time for that later."

She was torn between disappointment at not having *him* for breakfast and being thankful that there was actual food to consume. And coffee! "Coffee…" Sharon walked to the dresser to go over his tasty purchases. Absently, she said, "Thank you." After fixing the dark elixir of life just right, she sat in the desk chair and began to eat.

He sat at the edge of the bed, right across from her, and ate as well. He held his sandwich carefully, making sure no crumbs would fall to the floor. "Do you have plans for today?" he asked between mouthfuls.

"Does riding *you* count?" She winked at him with a grin, then took another bite.

He chuckled. "Yes, it does."

"In that case, I have two."

"And they are…?" he prompted.

"Well," she snickered, "you know one. The second is to catch up on work. I may not be able to show anything until I get back, but I can still hunt and schedule appointments." She sipped at her drink. "What about you?"

"I have only one plan. To steal you away."

"Ah ha!" Sharon exclaimed. "I knew you were too perfect." Using a napkin to clean her mouth, she teased, "I have to let you know that I won't go easily. I'll bite, and kick, and scratch." She clawed the air for emphasis.

"Come now, Shae," he argued, "you're in Vegas. You can't go to Vegas and spend your entire vacation in a hotel room working. It's not right."

Nervous laughter bubbled up and threatened to choke her. He was asking her to break habits that were ingrained in her soul for years. To stop *being* Sharon

Sampson. It was one thing to enjoy an evening off, or even a full day once in a while. But she would be gone for five days. And the others would be gone even longer.

Back at the office, her father was the only one handling calls and pushing things out until her return. Before leaving, Sharon had planned everything meticulously. Anything that needed an agent's presence was either done before their departure or scheduled for after their return. The only people who would need immediate attention were those who wanted to see properties and those who wanted to make an offer. Her father could handle that. Couldn't he?

Jon took advantage of her hesitation and pushed his plan. "Hey, what is a day in a bucket of thirty thousand?"

Confused, Sharon frowned. "What?"

Like a magnet, his black eyes pulled her gaze to his. "If you live to a little past eighty, you'd have approximately thirty thousand days of life." The intensity of his look, the passion in his voice, made her feel like she knew nothing. "Is it really worth it? To spend another one of those thirty thousand days working? Is your work so important that it cannot wait until your return home?"

Sharon was speechless. Those questions were intended to make her think, not only about that day, but her life as a whole.

Her work *was* important. She helped people and families find homes. Granted, sometimes she worked with businesses or landlords looking to make money, but that's what made the world go round, right? For the most part, she helped sell Suziq properties, so she was helping Sam.

VICTORIAN SURPRISE

   That's what she did—she helped people, one way or another.

   But was her help so essential that it couldn't wait another couple of days?

   I'm not a lawyer. Or a surgeon. No one's life is at stake, and no one I work with is homeless.

   Decision made, she grinned.

Vegas Night

Jon knew the exact moment she came to the same conclusion, that very little things in this world were ever that important. He saw it in her eyes, in her smile, but more in her body. Shae straightened her shoulders like a weight had been lifted. It was beautiful to see.

"Brilliant," he grinned.

"Okay," she shrugged inquisitively. "What do you have planned?"

"Nothing." It was his turn to shrug. "The point is to let go of plans, to be spontaneous. Let's just walk outside and see what happens."

For the next few hours, they walked the strip. They gambled, they shopped, they saw beautiful things and some things they *never* wanted to see. They talked and laughed, they shared stories and spoke of future dreams. The day passed far too quickly, but in a perfectly relaxed manner that they would both remember forever. By the time dinner ended, they were ready for full night's sleep. Still, they took their time walking back to Shae's room.

Standing just outside it, Jon asked, "Will you still be my plus one tomorrow?"

She locked eyes with him and padded his chest. "Yes, of course. It'll be fun."

"Good. I'm glad." Shae really needed to learn how to relax and let things go, to enjoy the moment. Having her with him will be good for everyone. She'll charm the pants off anyone she speaks to, and she'll have nothing to worry about. At least that was the plan. He was still a tad worried things could go awry. "I hope tomorrow goes superbly well. They deserve it."

"I'm sure it will, honey." After another tap, she turned to open her door.

"Yeah, for sure. It'll be lovely." Before leaving, he reminded her, "I'll be here at noon. Alright?"

"I'll be ready."

He gave her a quick kiss and left.

Getting Ready

Unfortunately, Sharon had only planned on attending one wedding, and so she had only one article of clothing that would be appropriate for such an occasion: a long, lavender gown that had a chiffon wrap over one shoulder. Considering her rather formal gown was intended for a maid-of-honor, she hoped it wouldn't pull away from the other guests attending.

After having breakfast with her family, she returned to her room for a shower and to change before Jon picked her up at noon. Suddenly, Sharon found herself standing in front of the mirror having second thoughts. Would she be crashing this wedding? Technically, she'd been invited, but not by either of the brides. With a sigh, she wrapped her hair in a tight bun, pinned it, and told herself if things got weird, she'd bail.

She was just about to apply her lip liner when she saw a couple of faded bruises on her neck, remnants of what she'd done with Jon. She bit her lip and wondered if she should hide them, either with makeup or her hair, but decided against it. Every time she looked in a mirror, she was reminded of how amazing her time with him had been. Who cared about what anyone else thought?

As if she'd conjured him simply by thinking of him, Sharon heard the knock on the door, and her breath caught when she opened it.

If she'd thought Jon looked handsome in a button-down shirt and slacks, she'd had no idea. Goodness, he

VICTORIAN SURPRISE

was positively edible in a tux. Her gaze was drawn first to his broad shoulders, which were clearly defined by the single button jacket he wore open, showing the waistcoat beneath. She didn't know how it was possible, but he looked even taller in the pleated trousers. The gray tie brought the whole outfit together and brought her eyes back up, where she noticed his still wet hair, slicked back, and his unshaven chin. Instead of having a clean face for the wedding, he had a short beard that made him look positively divine.

Immediately, she wondered how it would feel against her skin. Out of habit, she tried to tuck her hair behind her ear, but it was all pulled up in a bun. She pushed only a few wispy strays. Hoping he hadn't noticed, she grinned and bit her lip.

Jon's dark eyes were inscrutable. As his regard traveled the length of her, head to toes, his gaze had become hooded; his nostrils flared. "You look utterly dazzling."

"Ditto," she told him, her voice catching, breathless with desire.

Before he could tempt her, she left him in the doorway to return to the mirror and was surprised by what she saw. Apparently, lust was good for her. Her eyes were bright, especially with the dark makeup, and there was a natural blush in her cheeks. Her lips were full and rosy from her bite. *They might be even fuller with a kiss.* At that thought, they lifted on one side, giving her a mischievous look.

As she stood there, he came to stand behind her, and her insides dropped. They were stunning together. His dark hair and olive skin contrasted against her pale appearance. The black eyes, heavy with lust, against her own hungry look. *How far was it, to the chapel? Did they have enough time? Because, goodness, she was starving for him.*

Shaking away the dirty thoughts, she applied a lip stain that would stay with her for most of the day; a paler hue than her usual bright red, simply because her eyes were the focal point this time. And if the look Jon was giving her was any indication of the thoughts going through his mind, her choice was perfect. Maybe a little too perfect. "Stop looking at me like I'm your next meal."

"How can I?" Grabbing her upper arms, he leaned forward and kissed her exposed shoulder. Goosebumps erupted all over. "When you look so delectable." He scraped his teeth against her skin as he moved closer to her neck. "Positively scrumptious." Kissing and nibbling, his lips went to her nape.

Sensations shot through her and set her on fire. She closed her eyes and hissed, "If you keep doing that, we're never going to leave."

"That might not be a bad idea, love." His words were mumbled into the soft hairs on the back of her neck, causing her to shiver.

It was difficult to think when he drove her mad with lust, but she would feel terrible if he missed his best friend's wedding for a lay. Hard as it was, Sharon drew a quick breath and tried to ignore her tight, aching nipples. "Jon, honey…" she sighed, "your best friend is getting married."

Jon grunted, an unpleasant sound full of disappointment and frustration. Instead of releasing her, he wrapped his arms around her upper chest and pulled her closer. Nudging his face into the crook of her neck, he bit her there, sharply.

VICTORIAN SURPRISE

"Ouch!" She tried to sidestep, but he held on. Normally, she wouldn't mind a nibble or two, but this one was hard. Meeting his eyes in the mirror, she saw his crooked smile. "Is that my punishment for putting a stop to our morning delight?"

"Yes," he admitted. Sighing, he stepped back and let her go. "Are you ready, then?"

Her reflection showed a new bite mark was added to her neck, this one still bright red. She laughed, proud of the evidence of their time together. "Yes," she echoed.

They walked together to the elevator and waited patiently for it to arrive. While waiting, the memory of the last time they were in there together flashed in her mind. Sharon casually brushed nonexistent strands of hair from her face and tried to sneak a glance at Jon, only to find him already staring at her. The side of his mouth was raised and there was a hungry look in his eyes that mirrored hers, no doubt. She bit her lower lip and admitted that she was looking forward to a repeat. Grinning, they looked back at the elevator just as it dinged, announcing its arrival.

When the doors opened, they stepped in and turned to face the front, masking their disappointment at seeing another couple already there. Sharon sighed. It was for the best, really. If they had continued the way they were going, they would end up a mess; the telltale signs showing in rumpled clothing, messy hair, and smudged makeup. On the plus side, though, the waiting would make the experience so much better!

Once they stepped off the elevator, Sharon hooked her arm through his and they walked through the hotel lobby to a waiting limousine just outside. She went in first and as soon as he sat beside her, he linked his fingers through hers, just as he had done during their flight.

Looking at their joined fingers, Sharon's mind began to spin. It seemed like so long ago that he had sat next to her on the plane. She thought him odd then—and she still did, a little—but so much had changed in just a couple of days. Not in her life, she corrected mentally; things were still the same back home. But being with Jon made her *feel* different, like she was somehow stronger, freer. For the first time, she knew what it was like to feel free to be herself without constantly worrying about being judged; free from having to be the epitome of professionalism every minute of every day; free from having to put on a show for everyone around her. Because that's what she did when she was home—she acted.

Unconsciously, she shook her head in an attempt to throw the thought out, but it stayed.

For far too long, she'd been playing the role of real estate agent. Sharon loved her family, maybe a little too much because if she hadn't, she would have dropped that real estate hat a long time ago. But her father wanted her there, and both Scott and Sam needed her expertise.

Still lost in her thoughts, she looked out of the window, but didn't notice the bright, flashing lights of the Vegas strip. In her mind, she was seeing her calendar, and the mountain of stress that went with it. Scouting for land, staging properties, showings, inspections, closings, it was a never-ending circle of planning everything, to the smallest detail, while still staying flexible manage the inevitable surprises that went with every deal.

VICTORIAN SURPRISE

Sharon looked at Jon, saw how relaxed he was, how he was simply *in the moment* and smiled. Since that flight, she had taken his cue and lived in the moment. And so far, she had to admit, she loved it more than she could have ever imagined. Oh, there was still some planning; she couldn't just walk away from her family. But when she was with Jon, she felt honest enough to forget the rest of the world and enjoy life—and him. Every last delicious second she spent with him was full of uncomplicated pleasures and laughter. This would be a trip she would never forget.

With that thought came another: would she ever be able to return to her old way of life now that she knew how living honestly felt?

Elegant Venue

The trip was quick. Or maybe seemed quick because of the thoughts trampling through Sharon's busy brain. Either way, they arrived at their destination.

As a way of gently bringing her back to the present, Jon raised her hand to his lips. The move distracted her away from her thoughts and she grinned at him. Even without words, this man had the most gentle way about him. It was difficult to think of him as an MMA fighter. She still wasn't convinced that wasn't a fib on his part.

Walking arm in arm, they entered the building and headed straight for the chapel.

Unlike Samantha's choice of a low key event, Jon's friend had far more luxurious tastes. The scent of real flowers, roses, welcomed them. Crystal chandeliers hung from high ceilings, giving the room an expansive feel, while thick carpeting softened their steps. Beautiful moldings highlighted the room, as did the comfortable seating arrangements scattered about. It was an elegant venue for a formal wedding.

Struck as she was by the setting, Sharon didn't noticed the attention their arrival had attracted until Jon led her to a group of people. Five sets of eyes followed them curiously and Sharon turned her real estate charm on. A decade of experience made the transition seamless. She smiled graciously as she straightened her back and squared her shoulders.

Each person Jon introduced received a warm touch of some kind and an individual comment. "A pleasure to meet you, Sandi," Sharon said to the first person she met. "I love your shoes. You'll have to tell me where you got them." For some, Jon offered her an opening subject and she just had to go with it. "Brian, I love cats. Later tonight, you and I will have to share pictures." There were two others to charm before she finished with the last. "No, Eric, baseball is not better than football." She really didn't have an opinion on either sport, but if that was what Eric liked to talk about, then that's what they'd talk about. After listening to his thoughts, she squeezed his forearm for a quick second. "Okay, at some point tonight, you and I are going to have a serious talk about this," Sharon said with a soft laugh and moved away.

After so many years, the performance had become second nature. These comments and touches would help her recall their names and their story. People loved to feel special, and little things, like knowing which sport someone preferred, were what helped to make her a successful agent. She remembered them, and they remembered her.

Apparently, she was on the job even when she wasn't working. *Oh well*, she thought with a sigh.

Once the introductions were out of the way, Jon excused himself to go find Aly. Sharon watched him go and found herself wishing she could accompany him. Not that she was uncomfortable chatting with the folks who stood with her, she'd just rather spend her time with someone who made her lose focus.

And he did make her lose focus. As she watched him walk away, everyone faded into the background. Her gaze zeroed in on his broad shoulders and how they tapered down to slim hips. His hair had dried to become a mop of curls that went wherever they wanted to go. She couldn't wait to run her fingers through them again. Eventually, though, he turned a corner and she lost sight of him, forcing her to return her attention to the group. For the next half hour, she chatted with them and others who had arrived, while they waited for the brides.

Al's Phone

"You are..." Jon paused to get the right word. The beauty he saw before him was so vastly different from the woman he knew. She positively radiated with warmth and love. He shook his head and said, "You know, it's not fair." Putting his hands in his pockets, he raised his chin in defiance and mocked her with a dramatic sigh. "I've always known you were gorgeous, even when we were in school. It took me eons to get you to just go out with me. And after all the time I invested in you, you never looked as brilliant as you do now," with an exaggerated eye roll, he finished with a flair, "for *her*."

Eyes lit with laughter, Al played along and said, "Aw, you think I'm gorgeous?" She walked up to him and tugged on his lapels before flatting them down with her palms.

She certainly was. Instead of a veil, her hair was pulled back on the side with a flower clip; the rest fell to frame her beautiful face. The sleeveless dress flattered her breasts and waist with pleats, then dropped to the floor without the poof that so many gowns had. It was as simple and elegant as Al herself. Looking down at her, he answered truthfully, "You are exquisite, Al." Seeing the pleasure reflected on her features as a result of his words, he had to joke. "It's just too bad you play for the wrong team."

Her response was to slug him on the arm while laughing. "Maybe for you." She walked away from him and grabbed her phone, the fabric of her dress swooshing behind her.

It was good to see her so bright and happy. The shadows he had seen in her eyes were still there but had faded some, replaced with hope and the promise of a future spent with the love of her life. Jon worried that their time together wouldn't be very long, but he wouldn't dare comment, not on their wedding day. Why dull their happiness with the morbid thought that may or may not come to pass? They, better than he, knew what they were in for.

Oblivious to his thoughts, she continued. "Have you seen what penises look like? They're so ugly."

Jon cupped his hands protectively in front of his zipper and spoke directly to the offended member, "Don't listen to her, Stanley. She's an idiot."

"Am not!" She played with her phone and said, "Wait a minute and I'll show you." With purposeful steps, she walked over to him, about to show him something on her phone as he backed away.

"Seriously, Al?!" Laughing, he continued to back away while she followed, the phone aimed at his face. "What is wrong with you?!" He plucked it from her hands and held it above her head, just out of reach.

"Give it back!" she demanded while stretching for it.

"You want me to look at pics, yeah?" Still holding it high, he swiped through the screen. "Let's see what pics we have here." He turned it so Alyssa could see he was about to click on the photo album icon on her phone. Turning it to face him again, he pretended to go into it. "Oh, lookie here. Emily is quite lovely." He let out a low grumble of appreciation.

VICTORIAN SURPRISE

"So help me God, Jonathan Rossi," she threatened, her voice filled with anger. "Didn't your mother teach you to never go through other people's phones?!"

"Wait, you're quite upset about this." He would never violate her privacy, but it was just too funny, seeing her so flustered, to let it go. He gave in to temptation and enjoyed it. Still holding her phone high, he gloated, "There *are* pics of you two in here... together, *together*. Oh, such wicked deliciousness!"

Still reaching with one hand, she struck his kidney with the other.

The hit was executed well and he felt a momentary appreciation for the pain. "Damn," he said hoarsely while lowering his arm. Instinctively, he covered the wounded area, making it easy for her to take her phone back. Grinning, he said, "I taught you well."

"You're going to pay for that," Aly said while looking at it. Giving him a sideways glance, she frowned thoughtfully. "Who's that girl that came with you again?" With a wicked gleam in her gaze, she pursed her lips. "Shae, wasn't it?"

This would not bode well for him.

Jon was about to interject and sooth her over when she laughed and turned around, saying, "Yeah, I think we're going to be best friends."

"Oy!" Jon remembered just how many stories Alyssa could share and he experienced a real moment of fear. "There's no need for that, love. I didn't see anything." He walked around to face her and gave her a hug. "I was just being funny, you know."

"My relationship with my fiancée is not a joking matter, Jonathan." Through her words, he heard her laughter even though she pretended to be offended. She knew him too well.

"Honestly now," he said still holding her close. "Can you blame me? You two are exquisite apart. I can only imagine how wicked you are together."

He felt her shake her head and her chuckle was muffled into his tux. "You are such a *man*. Why do I even bother talking to you?"

"Because you love me, remember? And we have history." He squeezed harder. "I stood by you when you needed to hide from your parents. I'm always there to help you eat a pint of ice cream. You've tortured me with romantic comedies—so many of them, I've lost count. I'm the best mate you've got and better, since I've got muscle when you need to move."

Still wrapped in his arms, Al tapped his back and mumbled, "Yeah... I'm still going to have a few chats with your friend Shae."

Jon embraced her a little tighter. "Come now, Al," he told her, his chin resting on the top of her head, "do reconsider." Joking with her, he squeezed tighter still, until he knew the hug bordered on uncomfortable.

"Two can play that game, you know," she told him, her words muffled against his tux. Pulling back just enough, she wormed her hand between them and poked his chest with a single finger, hard.

"Bollocks!" Why did he have to teach her so well? Pulling back to rub the sore spot, he asked, "Has anyone ever told you that you're a tad violent?"

Unperturbed, she danced out of his forced hug with a laugh. "Only when people piss me off, Jonathan."

Just at that moment, someone knocked on the door. Immediately, Jon went to answer, and a staff member came in with a bright smile. "It's time." She nodded encouragingly to the bride. "Are you ready?"

VICTORIAN SURPRISE

Jon and Aly shared a look, a thousand thoughts and emotions exchanged without a single word spoken. Even if they hadn't known each other for the past almost twenty years, he would recognize them on her expressive face: anticipation, excitement, joy, eagerness.

Taking one last look in the mirror, Alyssa ran her hands over her hair, fixing nothing, then over her dress, straightening what was already perfect.

"Alyssa," Jon went to her and grabbed both of her hands, turning her to face him. When her bright eyes finally fixed on him, he tried to set her at ease. "You are lovely." Bobbing his head a bit, he continued, "I'm also fairly sure that Emily would marry you in a potato sack, so…" His voice trailed off with a shrug.

"So I have nothing to worry about," she finished for him. With a grin and misty eyes, she grabbed her bouquet and linked her arm through his. Together, they left the room.

Halfway down the hall, they saw Emily with her father walking in their direction. She was as beautiful and radiant as his Alyssa. The lacy veil was wrapped tightly around her bald head creating the illusion of long, pale tresses, and the rest of the fabric was placed to fall over her shoulder. Her dress, also made of lace, began at her neck like a choker and hugged her body to her waist, but left her arms bare. The bottom skirt consisted of light material that floated around her legs, revealing cuts in the fabric that went all the way up to her thighs. Sexy.

Knowing she would understand his tactic, Jon leaned over and whispered, "Are you sure I can't have her?" If he didn't give her something to laugh at, she would be sobbing in a moment. Jon knew her well enough to never let that happen in public. Not again, anyway.

A tap on the forearm she held was his answer. He took it as a non-verbal thanks for giving her some funny material.

"Well, I can't have *you,*" he persisted.

"Shut it," she hissed back, her voice lifting with the humor she was trying to smother.

He managed to sneak one last comment under his breath before the others were too close. "Greedy."

At that, she chuckled.

Just then, the four of them assembled at the entrance to the chapel, as happy as could be. Oblivious to their audience, the two women stared at each other with a blend of wonder and love.

Releasing Jon, Alyssa reached out to her fiancée and whispered, "Wow."

"Yeah," Emily responded, her voice breathless as she pulled from her father to accept Alyssa's hand.

As had been previously planned, the two men would be leaving them there and the two brides would be walking the short aisle together. No one would be giving anyone away, not in the traditional sense. The two of them had stood together for a long time and would continue to walk their journey together, including this path to their vows.

Turning to Jon, Alyssa said, "Thank you. For everything."

He leaned in and kissed her cheek. "I love you, Al." Before pulling away, he dropped one last quip and whispered quickly, "I want video of the wedding night."

Before she could respond, Emily's father turned to her and said, "I love you, kiddo." He kissed her gently on the cheek, then turning to include Alyssa, he added, "I can't wait for this to be official. Go get it done."

VICTORIAN SURPRISE

Before both men went into the chapel to take their places, Jon gave Emily a quick peck too. He stood at the altar as best man to the bride and swept his eyes through the room, glad that the guests had filled both sides instead of just Emily's. Toward the front, he saw Sharon, grinning and happy to be there. Their eyes met and her smile faded, became softer somehow. He was happy that he'd asked her to come.

Canon in D began as the two women started their march, holding hands with fingers linked, their bouquets in opposite hands. It was a perfect way to announce their union to the world.

Land Boats

Four tables were set up for the small wedding, and being Jon's plus-one, Sharon had the privilege of sitting with the brides. Not that the other guests were far; they were close by and they had the room to themselves. The thirty-some guests took full advantage and yelled over each other's heads to speak with a guest at another table without a second thought, laughing gaily and thoroughly enjoying every moment.

Sharon was surprised at how much fun she was having. Despite being a stranger, everyone present welcomed her as another family member. They included her in conversations, shared their stories with her, listened when she shared hers, and made her feel like she was one of their own. It wasn't long before her act dropped and she behaved like she would with her brothers and with Jon. Perhaps it was *because* of him.

There was something about that man. She didn't fully understand it, but when Jon looked at her, he drew honesty from her, allowed her to reveal the person she was at her core. Those black eyes of his saw everything and it didn't matter if these people liked Shae or not, *he* did. He inspired her to be open, encouraged her to speak her heart, and somehow made her feel that she could ignore the fear of how it would be received. Eventually, the persona that had become Sharon Sampson, real estate agent, momentarily disappeared and Shae shone through without filters.

VICTORIAN SURPRISE

"Land boat? Seriously?" Shae asked dubiously, looking at Jon sitting beside her. He, in turn, was looking at Alyssa, the evil gleam in his gaze telling everyone that she was going to pay for her outrageous disclosure.

"Seriously," Al confirmed. Sucking air between gales of laughter, she tapped the table and leaned back in her chair. Barely able to speak, she continued, "he was so drunk, he told everyone he needed to save it and get it home to the water. That it was wrong to keep it in a driveway, tied to somebody's truck. The worst part about all this? He had just made detective. Can you imagine it? I can see the headlines: *New Detective Rescues Neighbor's Boat.*"

Shaking his head, Jon asked, "Why do I put up with you?"

Shae was so happy she'd decided to come. She was learning so much about Jon, probably more than he ever wanted her to know, but she was having so much fun. Someday, she'd have to ask him all about being a detective.

Aly needed a moment to recover and catch her breath before answering him. She rested the heel of per palm on her chin and teased, "Because you love me." With a grin, she continued, "Admit it. I add sparkle to your life."

"Sparkle?" he questioned with an exaggerated frown of doubt. "More like sparks."

Everyone at the table laughed.

"Enough of you two," Emily said, grinning. She stood up and offered her hand to Aly, who quickly accepted. "I'm going to steal my wife away for a dance."

To their retreating backs, Jon yelled, "Good. She's a twat!" That earned him barely a glance over her shoulder. Instead, Alyssa focused on the dance, and after a while, others began to join them.

Still seated, Shae enjoyed the easy way Jon and Al joked with each other and smiled to herself. Clearly, they loved each other. They had a relaxed chemistry built on years of mutual support; had inside jokes that only those who were really close shared; and they were able to insult each other without any true harm. If she didn't know Alyssa was gay and happily married, she might have felt a twinge of jealousy.

The notion gave her pause. Funny that she thought she had any claim to him when they would part ways after their flight later that night. Maybe someday, once things settled in the office, they could get together again.

All of a sudden, the reality of what would be waiting for her when Sharon returned home weighed on her. Even with Sarah's help, the business was far too busy for the small number of agents they had. With Sarah and Scott both gone for a week and a half, Sharon would be struggling with her clients and theirs. A deep sigh escaped her.

Unexpectedly, Jon's arm wrapped around her shoulders and he pulled her close to whisper in her ear, "Come now, Shae." His breath tickled the loose hairs at her temple and goosebumps danced across her skin. "Forget whatever's going through your mind and enjoy the moment. Dance with me."

How she wanted to. It was easy to forget everything when he was so close. Easier still when he leaned in to kiss her neck, a quick tease that promised so much more if she let him. Torn between worrying about something she couldn't control and allowing herself to enjoy the moment, as he put it, Shae decided to put the future in

VICTORIAN SURPRISE

its place. Giving him a sideways glance, she thanked him with a smile. "Okay."

He stood up and offered her his hand, pulling her up when she took it. Once again, Shae forgot the world and her focus zeroed in on the man who looked at her with eyes so black, she could see her reflection in them. He led her to the dancefloor and spun her around in a wide circle before pulling her close.

Grinning like a fool, she enjoyed every second of their dance, and even more when the music slowed with the next song and she was able to close her eyes. Resting her chin on his shoulder, Shae felt his strong body against hers, felt the heat of his touch, heard the beat of his heart. Who knew being a guest at a stranger's wedding could have become one of the best days of her life?

But even the best of things had to end.

Still swaying to the music, Shae pulled back and said, "I need to go finish packing." There wasn't much, but she had to change and grab her makeup.

She watched his eyes roam her face and the easy way his lips lifted. Somehow she knew he wasn't ready to go just yet.

"So responsible of you," Jon teased.

"Some of us have no choice, you know."

"Yes, but," he gave her what would have been a somber look if he could've pulled it off without those laughing eyes, "some of us just don't know how to let go."

The song changed and the music picked up in tempo. Instead of leaving, they simply readjusted and continued dancing, their steps taking them around the floor, drawing the attention of everyone present.

Oblivious of their audience, she challenged him, "Are you calling me prissy, Jon?"

Without missing a beat, he responded, "Not in so many words, Shae." He lifted her arm and sent her into a spin, their moves so natural, they appeared to be choreographed.

When she returned to his arms, she said, "You know we have to leave." He shrugged. "I thought you said you were a martial artist. Aren't you guys taught self-discipline?"

"I've got plenty of discipline," he replied while pulling her even tighter, "and stamina."

She couldn't deny him that; she'd had first-hand experience in that department. "Yes, well," she stammered. As much as she'd love a repeat of his proficiency and control in that regard, she had to be on a flight in a few hours. Teasing him, she said, "That's quite a claim, but I can't test it right now. I have a red-eye to catch." After another spin, she corrected. "*We* do." The music ended and Sharon pulled back.

"Whatever your pleasure," he resigned with a sigh, "but for the record, it is not mine."

Gentleman that he was, he offered her his arm and they made the rounds to the other guests, wishing them well with some handshakes and many hugs. When they reached the brides, they stopped for a time and exchanged promises to meet up once everyone was home. It was a vow Sharon could happily agree to. They were funny, sweet, and so endearing, it would be no struggle to chill with them.

But for today, being so personable had taken its toll on Emily. Though still very happy, there were lines of strain on her face, and the broad grin she wore a few hours ago had faded a bit.

VICTORIAN SURPRISE

In a tone soft enough that only the four of them could hear, Jon asked, "Would you like me to tell them you're ready to go?"

Alyssa looked at her bride and waited for her decision.

"Thank you, Jon," Emily began, "for making this the best, most memorable day I could have ever dreamed of. You picked the perfect place." She gave him a wan, and very tired, smile. "I think it would only be fitting for you to end it since you started it all."

Sharon was shocked. This had been *his* doing? He had handled what was traditionally a bride's job and had done a beautiful job of it. The venue was elegant and everything had gone as smooth as silk. She looked at him in a new light. He was a surprising man.

"Truly, Em, it was my pleasure." They exchanged a hug. Turning to the rest of the group, he bellowed, "Hey, settle down buggers." Once the room had quieted and all eyes were on them, he continued, "The ladies have had enough of your appalling behavior and will be retiring. Continue forth with your mayhem if you wish but these two ladies will have no more of it." In unison, the group stood and came to them in a wave of bodies. Jon and Sharon quickly sidestepped before they got trampled.

Once they were safely out of the way, he told her, "If you wait here, I'll go grab my bag from upstairs and we can head to your hotel for your things, yeah?"

Her mind was still on the wedding itself. "Wait." He looked at her questioningly. "You did this?" With a wave of her hand, she encompassed the room.

He frowned. "The wedding?"

"Yes," she nodded.

Jon replied dismissively, "Well, yeah. Someone had to, and I was the only one really available. Em is going through treatments and Al is taking care of her. Besides," he shrugged with a grin, "I'm the best mate. It's my job."

What an amazing man. "This was really beautiful. You make an excellent wedding planner." Teasing him again, she gave him an impish grin. "Maybe I'll call you to handle mine, when the time comes."

"Ha!" he joked with her. "I feel for the poor bastard that gets stuck with you. You bite." He began to walk away before she could respond, and sent his last remark over his shoulder. "Literally."

Laughing, she shrugged. *Only during sex.* She would have told him that if he weren't already out of sight.

While she waited, she watched the others. Emily had said this was the best moment of her life and Sharon could understand why. She was surrounded by family and friends who wanted nothing more than to see her happy. They were getting the happily-ever-after everyone wanted, including Sharon. She sighed. Yet another couple going before her.

Alyssa didn't have her biological family with her, forced to hide her relationship as she'd had to, but appeared ecstatic with the new family that had embraced her. The guest list may have been on the smaller side, but the love in the room overflowed. She'd been to enormous affairs and hadn't felt half of the positive emotions as poured from these thirty-some people. Sometimes, family by choice was far better than blood relatives.

Unexpectedly, Sharon thought of her own mother, and her heart ached. She wouldn't have cared if she'd been gay; Sharon had no doubt that she would've been loved just the same. Her father would've grumbled a bit in the beginning but he loved his children to a fault, too. Case in point: Samantha. Sharon snickered. Back when her mother had been around, the tough-love of their father had been offset by her mother's caring nature. Now, he was just a grouch.

Melancholy wrapped around her. Though she was pretty sure that everyone who knew Susanne Sampson missed her too, they didn't miss her like *Sharon* missed her. The two of them had been very close when she was younger, inseparable sometimes. To Sharon, she had not only been a mother figure, but someone with true unconditional love; she had been a friend, a confidant, and an ally against the males when they drove her nuts, father and brothers.

In her mind, Sharon heard her voice, *Oh, that Jon is sooo cute! You did well, baby girl.*

Sharon reminded her imaginary mother that she had no time for relationships, especially now that the office was down to only two agents—again!—no matter how much she'd love to enjoy Jon's discipline and stamina.

Baby, I know your father has become even more of a grump since I've been gone, Sharon imagined her mom saying, *but I taught you to stand your ground. Those Sampson men are stubborn and, if it were up to him, your father wouldn't change a thing. Hell, he'd probably pull me from the afterlife, just so that I could keep cooking his steaks.* Sharon laughed softly. It was true; if he could've, he would've. *You tell him you want out. Trust me, baby, he loves you. And when he knows how unhappy you are, he'll fix it. Besides, this is driving Scott and Sarah nuts, too. Do it for all three of you.*

Even though she had been gone for almost four years, Sharon's mother still encouraged her, still pushed her to do the right thing, for herself and for others. *I'll do my best, mom.*

Sam's Neighbors

Sharon was lost in thought and didn't notice Jon's return. Jolted back to reality, she startled when he walked in front of her. Sweeping loose strands of hair away from her face and worrying her lower lip, she avoided his eyes but not before he noticed how watery they were. Concerned, he ran a soothing hand down her arm. "Everything all right, love?"

"Yes, fine," she answered evasively. Faking a smile to hide the threatening tears, she turned and began to walk purposefully toward the exit. But try as she might to hide it from him, Jon knew something was wrong.

It didn't take him long to catch up with her and he stepping in front of her, he blocked her path. She stopped and looked forward, staring at his lips. He wanted to know what was going on, but her behavior was eerily similar to Al's at the restaurant. Now would not be the time to force a conversation that may result in tears. Instead of pushing the issue, he offered her his arm and they walked out together.

Once in the car, they remained silent. She rested her elbow on the car door and her whole body faced away from him, as if she couldn't wait to run into the street the moment the door opened.

Jon had no idea what happened while he'd been away, but he had no problems reading the body language. Did one of the other guests mention something that put her on edge? It couldn't possibly have been more than fifteen minutes, and when he'd left her, she'd been laughing. What could have happened in that time?

"Shae." He called but she didn't respond. "Shae," Jon called again, this time a little more forcefully.

"Hm?" She looked at him as if she was surprised to see him there. It pleased him to note that her eyes were dry.

"I'm cold," he told her with a tiny hint of a smile. "And lonely." He beckoned her to him with his hands, a request for a hug.

Surprising him, Sharon gave him a wan smile and went to him, laying her cheek against his chest and sliding her hands under his jacket. *Okay, so nothing* he *did wrong.* He kissed the top of her head and wrapped his arms around her shoulders, holding her close. They stayed like that for a time while Jon contemplated whether or not to push her to talk. He decided against it when his shirt became wet with her tears. Seconds became minutes and still, she said nothing.

"Care to share, love?" he whispered into her hair.

"No," she mumbled against his chest.

They didn't speak again until the car stopped in front of her hotel. She straightened in her seat and rubbed her eyes. Looking at his shirt, she said, "I'm so sorry about that." Using one of the napkins in the car, she cleaned her nose.

"No worries, love," he told her. "It'll dry."

The driver opened the car door and they both headed inside. As they reached the elevator hallway, they saw Sam and Sam waiting for the next lift. *Of all the people in the hotel.* The brother looked at Shae and his face became thunderous when he saw the tear streaks. His eyes went to Jon immediately, and Sam stormed to him in seconds.

VICTORIAN SURPRISE

Bollocks! "Oy, mate," Jon said raising his hands passively.

"What the fuck did you do to my sister?" Sam demanded while grabbing Jon's tux.

Jon allowed himself to be pushed against the wall but gripped both of Sam's wrists, ready to spin them and break the hold if he tried anything else. Jon gave him points for defending his sister, but this shit was getting old.

"For fuck's sake, Sammy." Shae said as she stepped in and tried to push Sam back, to no avail. "I was thinking about Mom." Those last words were muttered softly.

The anger drained and turned to suspicion. Instead of releasing Jon, he looked at her, wondering if she was lying. Once he saw what he wanted to see, he stepped back.

At least now, Jon knew what the issue was. He would have rather gotten that information another way, though. Straightening his shirt and jacket, Jon followed the others and ignored the awkward silence echoing in the hallway. Somehow, he was going to have to talk to Sam about this. If he tried swinging at Jon again, the result would be unpleasant. Jon would make sure of it.

When the elevator arrived, the two women got on first, but the reluctant men held back, each wanting to be last. Samantha and Sharon looked at each other and shook their heads. Muttering under their breath, Samantha grabbed Sam's hand while Sharon grabbed Jon's, and they tugged the two men in at the same time. Samantha reached out and pushed the button, and when the doors opened on their floor, the women physically pushed the men out.

Sharon's room was first and the two Sams kept going while she opened the door to her suite. Before following Sharon in, Jon called to Sam and walked over to him. In a low tone for his ears alone, Jon told him, "Twice you've gone after me, and twice I've let you." He paused, letting the words sink in. "I won't hold back a third time." Jon watched as the threat hit home and the fury set in. "Got it, mate? Yeah?" He nodded for emphasis.

Sam's gaze went frigid and his eyes narrowed. "Yeah," he acknowledged, "sure." He made to walk away but then stopped, the appearance of having a second thought. A slow, cold and calculating grin curled his lips. "You know, you should stop by our house sometime. We could have dinner, then maybe, we could go for a walk outside and I could introduce you to the neighbors."

Jon had no idea where Sam lived but got the impression that it wasn't all that lovely. "Yeah. Sure, mate." Considering the murderous light in Sam's eyes, his dinner would probably be poisoned and his body thrown over a cliff or into a piranha-filled lake. Either way, Jon made a mental note to never accept a dinner invite from either Sam.

Just Heels

The door swung shut behind her too quickly and Sharon realized Jon hadn't followed her in. Worried about another fight, she went to check, but Jon was standing by the door, hand raised to knock. Sticking her head out, she could see Sam down the hallway, letting himself into his suite. Relieved, she stepped back.

"May I come in?"

"Of course."

They both looked around, but there wasn't much to pack. Sharon put her clothes back into her suitcase. The laptop was already stored away. The only things left were her toiletries. Before she started on those, she decided to change out of her gown.

All of a sudden, she was acutely aware of Jon, standing a foot away, looking edible as always. He had changed into another button-down shirt and she was tempted to undo those buttons slowly, one by one, until she exposed the hard chest beneath. Standing there, staring, she remembered the demanding pressure of his lips on hers, the warmth of his naked skin against hers, the sensation of his body sliding in and out of hers. Her breath caught and her heart pounded. Just thinking about it made her nipples tighten.

Just as she decided to act on her impulse, Jon grabbed her for an intense kiss. His hands framed her face as his lips devoured her mouth. When she opened it for him, his tongue swept in to taste her, one of those quick, teasing sweeps, the kind that sent her own tongue into his mouth because it hadn't been enough. Over and over again, they kissed. Between gasps for breath, their tongues danced and teeth nibbled on swollen lips. With eyes shut tightly, Sharon gripped his shirt and held on, lest she fall with the intensity of it.

She felt his beard as he purposely scraped it against her chin, savoring the way her body reacted to it: the spinning in her belly, the hardening nipples, the tingle between her legs.

Jon's hands moved to her hair and blindly, he pulled out the pins holding it in place. Dropping them to the floor, he released the chignon, and ran his fingers through the smooth, platinum strands, tugging lightly.

The sensation reminded her that she wanted to run her fingers through his dark tangle of curls, too. As he moved his kisses to her jaw and neck, she leaned back to give him better access, and grasped a handful of his hair to hold him in place.

She gasped for breath when he moved to grab a breast, hard, arching her back as he nibbled her neck, no doubt adding bruises to the three already there. Sharon tried to laugh at the thought, but it came out as a throaty moan, her body's way of letting him know how he made her feel: gloriously alive.

Goosebumps erupted on her skin when he pulled the dress up over her head. Absently, Jon let the lavender gown fall to the floor and focused his eyes on the satin bra and panties he wanted to remove next. Slowly, he peeled off one article of clothing at a time, first the lace trimmed bra, then the tiny matching panties. Closing his eyes, he savored the feel of her willing body in his hands, until at last, she was wearing nothing but her heels.

VICTORIAN SURPRISE

Once he had her naked, Jon settled his hands on her hips, kneading gently while Sharon struggled with the buttons of his shirt, her hands shaking with urgency, wanting the garment gone. When it finally gaped open, she ran her nails over his skin, loving how his eyes closed and his head dropped back. She quickly moved lower and undid his pants, slipping her hand in to feel the hard length of him.

As his pants dropped around his ankles, he said, "Enough foreplay, don't you think?" His voice was hushed and heavy, his dark eyes hooded with desire.

A small whimper of desperation was her only reply.

He moved back to toe his shoes off and, after taking a condom from his pocket, stepped out of the pants. Sharon plucked the condom from his hand. Quickly, she pinched the end and unrolled it firmly onto Jon's cock, making erotic little noises as she did. Condom in place, he scooped her up. Immediately, her arms went around his neck, just as her legs wrapped around his waist. Jon walked forward until her back was against the wall, and positioning her legs over his forearms, he slammed into her. Hard and fast. Sharon gasped at being so full so quickly. Their moans blended, quickly followed by short pants that echoed each thrust. Unable to keep silent, her cries filled the air.

Sensations overwhelmed her as her insides clenched around his cock. *Damn, he was big.* Looking for something to hold, she scratched his back before moving to cup his head, barely registering the feel of his hair curling around her fingers. Without stopping, he lifted her from the wall, changing the angle and hitting all the right spots. The pleasure built quickly, and within seconds, she was climaxing, her body trembling as waves of sensation and pleasure washed through her.

Soon after, she felt him shudder as he spilled himself, his growl of satisfaction music to her ears. Though how he could manage while still standing and holding her up, she didn't know. He took her to the bed then, gently laying her down before collapsing beside her, both of them weak and gasping for breath.

Minutes passed as they both stared at the ceiling, recovering. Eventually, Jon broke the silence. "If we're going to make the flight, we must leave soon."

Sharon rolled her head to look at him, smiling. "How soon?"

His dark eyes smiled back, still heavy and lazy. "Hmm…" he considered, "five minutes or so. Ten at most."

"Well, honey," she replied softly, "I'm halfway there."

"Are you now?" he mumbled with a laugh.

"Yup," Sharon grinned. "I've already got my shoes on." She raised both feet high as evidence, then laughed.

Turbulent Flight

The plane was rolling on the runway, about to take off, and Shae's anxiety was in full force. Jon could feel her heart racing as he rubbed her hand, pausing for a bit on her wrist to check her pulse, before rubbing her icy fingers again. Despite her fear, she insisted on staring out of the window, as if she could control the plane's trajectory simply by watching where it went.

He said the one thing guaranteed to get her attention. "Shae, I've been giving the idea some consideration, and I think you should help me find a place for my dojo." Not that it was a lie, per se. While he didn't think he needed help finding a location, he knew it was a subject she couldn't ignore.

Surprised, her head whipped around to face him, blue eyes wide beneath a frown. "Why?"

Not the response Jon was expecting. "Because it's been ages and I haven't found anything on my own," he admitted. "And you're an expert."

"Okay…" Her voice trailed off and she looked out the window again.

The plane took flight and, with eyes closed tightly, she gripped his hand for dear life.

When she didn't speak again, Jon pressed. "Have you changed your mind about helping me?"

Her eyes remained shut and her frown deepened. "Of course not," she retorted. "I'd love to help."

Jon got the impression that she was insulted by his question. Either that, or she was getting annoyed with his constant pestering. His distraction tactic was working.

The plane steadied and she finally looked at him. Tugging her hand away, she added, "We should schedule a time to discuss the details when I'm in the office we can go through the available listings together."

This plan of his might backfire. After all, this was her business. He didn't want to lead her on, when all he wanted was her attention. *What the hell.* He could always cancel after they landed. "Whatever your pleasure, love," Jon grinned. "But perhaps we could go through them over dinner, yeah?"

"Jon," Shae gave him that sweet but apologetic smile, the one women gave when they were about to reject a suitor. "I know we've had a wonderful time together these past few days and honestly, I've loved every minute of it. But I have a business to run, and now with two agents out of the office, I will barely have time to breathe." She reached out and squeezed his fingers. "I'm swamped on an average day," she explained, "never mind now."

"Very well," he said, trying to sound only slightly disappointed, "we'll go through the listings in your office." After a pause, he inclined his head. "Then, we'll go to dinner."

With a barely perceptible shake of her head, she laughed and pulled her hand back. "You're incorrigible."

"What?" he asked with an exaggerated frown. "Agents don't eat?"

"Of course we eat," she confirmed. "We eat in the car... between showings." After a pause, she finished, "When we remember."

VICTORIAN SURPRISE

"That can't possibly be healthy," Jon muttered. *No wonder she's so slender.*

"Eh…" She shrugged, resigned to the situation she was returning to.

Since there was nothing he could do about that, he decided to let the matter drop. "So…" Jon said into the silence that had stretched. "We are, once again, trapped in a flying can with not much to do. How do you propose we pass the time?" His eyes bright with laughter, he offered, "Shall we discuss politics? Religion? There is the ever-popular subject of climate change."

She chuckled softly and gave him a sideways glance. "Those are all very… interesting choices, but since we're stuck on a plane and I don't want to," she lowered her voice to a whisper before continuing, "start a political argument with the other passengers," her tone returned to normal, "I'm going to pass."

"Aw, come now," he pouted, "it'll be a long flight if we don't chat about something." Looking up at the ceiling of the plane, he gave the matter some thought and came up with the most brilliant idea. With a wicked grin, he offered, "unless you want to head to the bathroom and join the mile-high club." He winked.

"That is a—"

Her words cut off abruptly when the plane jumped and seemed to drop from beneath them. Shae's terror returned swiftly, expressed in her wide eyes and frightened gasped. She bit her lower lip so hard, he was surprised she hadn't drawn blood. Her hands gripped the arms of her chair until her knuckles were white.

"Hey, now," Jon said soothingly. "Just a bit of turbulence."

Lena Lane

The captain came on the speakerphone then, making them feel simultaneously better and worse. "We've hit a bit of a storm, so expect some turbulence for the next several minutes. Please stay seated and make sure your seatbelt is secure."

The plane shook and jarred them back and forth, before dropping again. It was enough to make Jon feel uncomfortable, but for Sharon, it was the stuff of nightmares. Frantically, her gaze jumped from the window that reflected nothing but darkness, to the seats in front of her, then side to side, and up to the ceiling, before returning to stare out the window again. In seconds, she had seen everything that could be seen from her seat and still she looked desperately for something that could give reassure her.

Jon twisted in his seat, as much as the belt would allow, and ignored the dig of the armrest against his thigh. "Shae, look at me." He placed his hand on hers to bring her attention to him, but her eyes remained unfocused. "Look at me, Shae," he repeated more insistently, gripping her icy fingers tightly. "Shae!" With his free hand, he grasped her chin and forced her to look at him. Finally.

Blue eyes filled with terror, she was hyperventilating. She gasped for air and the pulse at her wrist was racing. "Jon," she whispered in panic, "What do I do?!"

"You look at me, love." He gave her a gentle smile. "You look at me and tell me a story." *Anything to get you to stop thinking about where we are.* With one hand, he made gentle circles on her wrist with his thumb, and with the other, he stroked the hair from her face, tucking the strands behind her ear. He hoped the different touches would distract her.

Shaking her head, she frowned at him. "What?"

VICTORIAN SURPRISE

"Tell me a story." He kept his voice calm while still caressing her wrist and cheek. "Anything will do," he encouraged calmly.

"That's not going to help, Jon!" she practically yelled at him, not that anyone around them cared. The shaking plane was making enough noise to drown out most everything else.

Good, he thought. *If she's angry at me, she won't think about anything else.*

Nice Distraction

A story?! I'm about to die and he wants me to tell him a story?! As if compelled, she began to share an incident from when she was in the fourth grade. There was a Thanksgiving play. Each student in her class was dressed as a traditional Thanksgiving dish and had a line to recite about it. Sharon was dressed as mashed potatoes. She recalled walking out onto the school auditorium stage with her classmates, but for the life of her, she couldn't remember what she said on stage. "What do mashed potatoes say, exactly?"

"Um… not something I can answer, love, I wasn't there." Jon tried to swallow his laughter, but she could hear it anyway, and for a fleeting moment, a small smile crossed her lips.

When she began to worry her bottom lip again, he reached out and traced it with his thumb, rubbing it gently. His hand moved slowly to wrap around her nape before he pulled her forward. Time slowed when she noticed the desire in his gaze. Distracted, she forgot where she was and closed her eyes, waiting for the kiss she knew was coming.

The only thing Sharon could focus on was the soft pressure his lips made against the side of her mouth. And again, when he kissed the other side. The kisses were off center, and gentle, soothing her bruised lips, and somehow they reached her soul and drove the fear away. They were so feather-light that she wondered if she imagined them. But then, he kissed her again. And again. Sweet and gentle, he kissed the upper lip. And then the bottom. Over and over, he brushed his lips against hers so softly, it was beginning to drive her mad. She'd had enough of these off-center pecks.

She grabbed his shirt, pulled him close, and kissed him roughly. Holding him in place, she bit his lower lip and swept her tongue into his mouth. The world shook with the intensity of it. Needing air, she pushed him away and gasped for breath. When she looked at him, she saw the same raging need in his dark gaze, mirroring her own. Her belly swirled and her insides clenched, wanting him inside her.

With heavy eyes, his gaze roamed over her face: her eyes, her cheeks, her lips, and chin. There was no doubt he saw the lust she felt for him. She felt exposed again. He knew her secret, how much she wanted him, her hunger. But right now, she didn't care. All she cared about was how he made her feel. And it was amazing.

Ignoring the eyes of the passengers who sneaked glances at them, or others who watched with undisguised curiosity, Sharon pulled Jon close again and renewed their passionate distraction. *Let them watch.*

Separate Ways

Jon had no idea how much time they spent with their lips locked, but his tactic for distraction worked like a dream. And a very pleasant dream it was. If only they were in private and could continue. But like everything else, it had to come to an end, this time, with an annoying voice through the plane speakers.

"Ladies and gentlemen," the pilot reported, "we have arrived at our destination—" His voice prattled on, but neither Jon nor Shae heard him. His attention was on her, and her attention was focused on the lights outside the window. Once again, she was trying to control the plane by sheer force of will. He almost laughed out loud.

Soon enough, the plane made a perfect landing and Shae began to breathe normally again.

Immediately, the people around them began to pull their things down from the storage compartments overhead, but Jon and Shae stayed where they were, unwilling to leave just yet. They ran out of time when the doors opened and people began to file out.

"Home sweet home," he said, breaking the silence. As he watched, she took a deep breath and exhaled slowly. The action reminded him of someone meditating. *No*, he corrected quickly, *she's looking for courage.* He wondered what kind of battle she was preparing herself for; whatever it was, it wasn't going to be pretty.

VICTORIAN SURPRISE

She puffed out. "Yeah, something like that." With that, she squared her shoulders and stood up.

Following suit, he stood and reached for their bags. Once he had them in hand, he motioned for her to go ahead of him.

Shae was quiet, and he imagined her making a mental list a mile long, of things she had to get done before sunrise. Her distress didn't stop him from watching her ass as she walked down the ramp ahead of him. He let himself enjoy her silhouette until the path opened up to the airport and they could walk side by side.

From the corner of his eye, he saw her sneak a quick look at him as she said, "You have my card, call me."

"Sure, love." At this point, though, he didn't know if he would. He had a lot of work to do, and so did she. Not wanting to leave her on such a sad thought, he joked with her, "You know, you can't go around telling people you don't bite."

Another quick look; this time with a real smile. "Well, you're the exception to the rule. My first, my only." Her head quirked a bit and she swept her hair from her face, her long, red nails catching the light as she did. "But since I know how well it worked, I might have to do it again." She winked at him. "Later."

He laughed softly as they went their separate ways.

Old Habits

Old habits die hard. Or in this case, they never died at all. Having been partners for so long, each knew how the other behaved, knew how to play off each other, knew how to keep each other safe. Without comment, both men got their drinks from the counter at the coffee shop, then made their way to a corner booth. They sat against the wall, keeping a clear view of everyone in the shop, which included an uninterrupted sight of the door. Each person coming in, and leaving, was accounted for and evaluated for potential risk.

After sitting, Jon felt the old man's eyes on him, appraising him, assessing him, trying to determine what had passed in the time they'd been apart. Jon was guilty of doing it, too. Peter Leveque had aged some more. He could've—should've—retired long ago, but refused to quit the job he loved so much. Catching the bad guy was what he lived for.

Swinging his arm over the back of the bench seat, Pete used his typical sarcasm as an opening line. "Damn, Jon, you've really let yourself go." He took a sip of his drink. Immediately, his dark eyes swept through the small shop, always looking for things that shouldn't be. His once dark hair might be gray now, and his face may be lined with evidence of his age, but his gaze was still quite sharp.

"Yeah, Pete," Jon snickered, "and you're almost funny." He leaned back in his seat and did his own sweep. "I'm not the one whose shirt is about to pop."

VICTORIAN SURPRISE

Looking back, Jon purposely focused on the button down shirt his old partner wore. The fabric was stretched tight over the belly that had rounded out over the past few years; the button immediately above his belt barely holding on.

Pete scuffed. Swinging his arm forward, he held his cup between both hands. "What the hell is with your accent, man?" Pete asked. "You've been in jolly ole England a little too long? You've become a, ah… a British 'bloke'? Is that the word?" Laughing, he continued, "Or maybe it's a 'dandy'?"

Shrugging the comments off, Jon shook his head. Calmly, he said, "You know damn well I was there for years. It's hard to immerse yourself in a country and culture without picking shit up." While looking through the room again, a petite blonde walked in and caught his attention. She was beautiful—gorgeous, even—but he found himself thinking of another blonde. Tall, slender, with eyes so blue, they rivaled a summer sky in beauty. Bringing his attention back to Pete, Jon said, "Besides, the gals love it."

"Yeah, I bet they do." Changing the subject, Pete asked, "Have you started looking for your dojo yet?"

Jon swallowed the grin that threatened when he thought of Shae. Instead, he shrugged and said, "Not yet. So many bloody things to consider."

"Good luck with it." Pete brought his cup to his lips, but his eyes remained on the room at large. "Real estate has gone down the shitter around this area. The Mayor is seriously pissed about it." Putting the cup down, he threw his arm over the back of the bench again, stretching the shirt taut once more. "Agents aren't showing properties solo, and that just makes a difficult process worse."

"What do you mean?"

"They're going out in pairs."

That was concerning. Why would agents need to go out in pairs? Leaning forward, Jon rested his elbows on the table and questioned, "Why?"

"While you've been off getting your manly accent," he snickered, "there have been several reports of assaults and robberies, with agents being the primary targets. A guy shows up to look at a house, but he's got a partner the agent doesn't know about. While the agent is distracted with one, the other knocks 'em out." Letting out a deep breath, he said, "The men get robbed." His hand curled into a fist by his cup before he whispered, "The women get robbed and the bonus of being assaulted."

"Assaulted…?"

Pete looked Jon in the eye. "You know what I mean."

Jon was immediately worried for Shae, and his gaze locked on Pete's. "How long has this been going on?" He needed details. All of them.

"Since before Christmas last year." Shaking his head, Pete continued, "The Mayor doesn't want it on the news because sales are low to begin with. Now people are afraid of calling agents."

"What the fuck, Pete?" The words were hissed between clenched teeth. "Sha—" He caught himself before finishing her name. "Agents are getting assaulted and it's not on the news because sales might drop? And why are people afraid to call? It's the *agents* getting attacked." He gripped his drink so tightly, the cup bent; dark liquid poured from the top. Ignoring the spill, he fumed, "They should be made aware of these dangers."

VICTORIAN SURPRISE

"Settle down there, Jonny," Pete raised his hand to placate him. "They *were* made aware. That's why they're going out in pairs." Frowning, he asked, "What's your issue? Why are you so invested in this?" He looked around the room at large again before he challenged Jon, "You were the one who decided to leave the job, remember? You decided to walk away."

Rather than answering, Jon got up to compose himself. He wasn't about to tell his old partner that someone he cared about was a real estate agent. He walked to the counter to grab some napkins so he could clean the mess he made, and by the time he returned, he was back to his usual, calm self. Wiping up the spill, he said, "I'll never understand why money is more important than someone's safety. Does the Mayor not realize agents are people, too?"

Exasperated, Pete straightened in his seat. With tight lips, he replied, "I just told ya," each word carefully pronounced, "the department informed every office in the area. We sent them an email with precautions every agent should take to stay safe."

"An email…" Jon walked away to throw the dirty napkins in the trash. As he walked back to the table, he noticed his old partner's body language. His lips were tight with disapproval; his body rigid with tension; but worse, his eyes were narrowed with suspicion. It didn't matter. Shae's safety was more important than the old man's disapproval. *Some of us can't live with the darkness until we die.* "Fine, mate." Sitting back down, Jon asked, "So, what's being done about it?"

Grumpy Call

Two weeks. Two hellish weeks of not eating, not sleeping, not resting in any way. Two weeks of nothing but running around, of wishing for the end of the bull crap that was real estate. Sharon was so done. The next time her family decided to get married, and go off to Fiji or Vegas or anywhere else for their honeymoon, they'd have to find someone else to watch the office. *Because I am done. D. O. N. E. Done.* It was a good thing they were scheduled to return that night. Any longer, and they'd come back to burned ruins. The only reason she hadn't already dropped a lighted match into a trash can was because she wasn't sneaky enough to get away with it, and she looked horrible in orange.

Returning her focus to the task at hand, Sharon wondered whether she should pick up the newlyweds from the airport herself or send a car. By now, though, it was probably too late to schedule a pickup. *That's what you get for procrastinating.* But she already knew why she hadn't made arrangements sooner. Considering how much she was looking forward to putting her real-estate-hat down and just walking away for a bit, she couldn't wait to do what she had been wanting to do for so long. *Leave.* Sharon grabbed her bag and jacket, then left.

She was merging onto the highway when her phone began to ring, the sound echoing through her car's stereo system, jarring her from her peaceful silence. Groaning in frustration, she contemplated rejecting the call and sending it to voicemail. Probably someone calling about a showing; or a problem with an inspection; or some issue with a mortgage. It didn't matter if she tried to walk away from real estate—even for a minute. It followed her everywhere she went. Frustrated, she groaned.

While her thumb hovered over the reject button on her steering wheel, she sighed and took a quick peek at the caller ID on her dash. *Jon.* Seeing his name put a smile on her face. Not a big one; just a tiny lift at the corner. He was probably the only person that could make her feel better at this point in her life. But not even he could eliminate the drain she felt.

"Hey, stranger," she said in greeting.

The sound of his deep voice filled her car; his words still infused with the sexy accent she adored. "'Ello, love." She hoped he'd never lose it.

Until now, Sharon hadn't realized she had missed him, but she had. His charm, his humor, his easy manner. "How have you been?"

"Good," he said simply. "I've been getting settled in, catching up on some stuff for my family."

As he spoke, she noticed his voice didn't have its usual lighthearted tone and she wondered if something was wrong. It was then that she realized she'd been so focused on herself and on how he made her feel that she never found out anything about him as a person, as an individual. Shame crawled through her. She didn't know anything about his family, or his background, beyond the short conversations they had in Vegas. "How are they?"

"Fine." The answer was dismissive, almost brisk. The single word contained a sharpness she hadn't experienced from him before. It didn't invite further talk on the subject, so she said nothing. "I think I'm ready to move forward with the dojo now. The sooner, the better. Can we chat tonight?"

Damn it. Should've sent a car to pick them up after all. But it was too late. "I'd love to help, but I'm on my way to the airport right now. How about tomorrow?"

There was a short pause, and then he asked, "The airport? Are you heading somewhere?" He sounded distracted, distant. Unhappy. Where was the cheerful man she'd left two weeks ago? What happened?

"No," she said quickly. "Just picking up Scott and Sarah." Considering his tone, she decided that she would like to see him. Maybe she could help cheer him up. "But you know what? We should be back by eight. Would you mind coming to my place around eight-thirty?"

"No, no," the dismissal was clear, "I'm sure you'll be tired, love. This can wait until tomorrow." He was done, too. Done with what, though, she didn't know.

Part of being a successful agent was being able to read people. If she had learned anything over the years, it was how to discern information from the tone of someone's voice, or their body language, if they were face-to-face. What's being said, but more importantly, what's missing. And in this case, his voice was sharing more than he wanted44 to. "But I want to see you…" she admitted into the silence. Hopefully, her honesty would be enough to change his mind and he would want to see her too.

He snickered and said, "You should have taken that pic of us when you had the chance. Then you could see me anytime you wanted to." It must have worked. He sounded lighter, more relaxed.

"Ha, ha," she joked with him, "you're so funny." On a more serious note, she added, "You know it's not the same."

The silence stretched before he asked, "Miss me, do you?"

A couple of heartbeats passed before she answered, "Maybe..." Her voice drifted at the end, making it clear to him that she had. She was probably giving away more than she planned, but what the hell. She needed another escape from reality, and he was the perfect distraction.

"Well," he said, "what kind of gent would I be if I left you alone in your time of need?"

There he is, the man I've come to adore. "Gent?" Sharon asked, "As in gentleman?"

"Yes, of course." The British accent was even more pronounced. She had no doubt that he'd done it on purpose.

"Oh, honey," she mocked playfully, "you are no gentleman."

"Excuse me?!" He almost sounded genuinely insulted.

"Just because you pretend to be one, by speaking in that fancy accent, and dressing in those fancy clothes, that doesn't mean you *are* one. After all, I know what you did in Vegas." Memories of their time together came to tease her. Their walks, their dancing, their intimate moments. Those last ones were enough to make her stomach drop with lust.

"Vegas? What about Vegas?" he challenged, "I was a perfect gentleman, who came to your rescue, mind you. Do you remember that first night?"

Oh yes, she most certainly remembered their first kiss. A peck that lasted only a second, but left its mark just the same. Still, she wouldn't let him think she was some damsel in distress, needing to be rescued. "I would have been able to get rid of him." Sharon pressed. "Your presence just made things a little easier."

"Whatever you say, love," he mocked. "Text me your address and I'll see you later tonight."

"Will do."

She was about to end the call via her steering wheel, but he made one last comment, "Please be safe."

Sharon was touched by his words. Softly, she answered, "Always."

Be Safe

Nonchalantly, Jon walked around Shae's home. It was small but open and inviting. She had made it her own by filling it with warm furniture, paintings, and pictures of her family, but it was neat—almost too neat. Everything was in its place. It was then that he remembered she staged property for a living. He had a suspicion that it was all for show.

From the corner of his eye, Jon could see her at the kitchen table, her open laptop before her. But he was more focused on the apartment as a whole. Where someone lived told him plenty about the person who lived there.

In her case, it was easy to see that she loved the beach, since the focal point of the condo was an enormous painting of a beach scene. Also scattered across the walls were some stunning black and white architectural designs. Mostly though, she was surrounded by family. The walls and furniture were covered with pictures. Some of them were older, from when the three siblings were much younger. Others were newer, portraying current age. Jon was not surprised by any of this.

What almost surprised him was what he saw through the open doorway into her bedroom: the small bookcase full of romance novels, and the mess scattered through the room. Along with an unmade bed covered in laundry, and more laundry peeking from the side of the bed on the floor, there were empty plates, bowls, and glasses. Her dresser was covered in books and papers. He snickered softly as his suspicion was confirmed. The rest of the condo might be impeccable—and possibly staged for guests, but her bedroom was where she let herself go. That's where the real Shae lived.

Nonchalantly, he walked back toward the kitchen, before she caught him snooping around her house. She was so focused on what she was doing, however, that she was completely oblivious to his study. Just as he reached the table, she looked up.

"Please sit," she told him as she did the opposite, "I'm just going to go grab a notebook and pen." She headed for her bedroom.

While she walked away, he watched her and enjoyed her hourglass figure. Her shirt was tucked at her waist, emphasizing how tiny it was, while her slacks hugged her rounded hips. Her pale hair was tied up in some sort of twisted bun high on her head, leaving her neck exposed and begging for his lips. Or his teeth. Both? Oh, the delicious things he could do to her. He almost felt bad for thinking such dirty thoughts about his real estate agent, but not bad enough to stop.

When she returned from her bedroom, she closed the door behind her.

For the next hour, they discussed locations, cost, and features associated with different options for his dojo. They had a short list of places to look at, and she would schedule the appointments in the morning. A solid plan was in place.

"You know, love, I was such a bugger," Jon said as she closed her laptop, "you were absolutely right in saying that an agent would make this easier." Resting his elbows on the table, he leaned closer and smiled. "Thank you."

"You're very welcome, Jon." She too leaned forward, almost close enough to kiss. A small smile lifted the corners of her lips and her sky blue eyes sparkled with warmth. "I'm happy to help." There was no doubt she spoke the truth. She may not enjoy all aspects of the business, but at the very least, she liked helping people. Or at least him.

He watched her gaze drop to his lips and he grinned wickedly. With the business portion of the visit complete, perhaps they could move onto better, and far more entertaining, activities. Perhaps *all* the laundry will be strewn onto the floor before he left. He locked eyes with her and lowered his tone to almost a whisper when he flirted, "Are all agents as brilliant and lovely as you?"

"Oh no," she joked, maneuvering as close to him as she could while not crawling onto the table, "your agent is quite exceptional."

At that, Jon closed the distance between them. Their eyes met and soon, so did their lips. Still kissing, they both stood and he gently grabbed her at her waist. When she locked her hands behind his neck, he slid his hands down her back to her perfect ass and pulled her closer to him so she could feel how stiff he was. *God, she's amazing.* When he pulled back, he tugged at her shirt, craving the soft skin beneath.

Immediately, her hands went to his to stop him. Pulling back, she looked at him and breathlessly said, "No, not now." She closed her eyes and rested her head against his chest while she interlocked her fingers with his. Breathlessly, she mumbled against his shirt, "Not today."

Well, that sucks. He let out a grumble of disappointment. "Why not today?" He tried to be good but temptation won over. Releasing his hands from hers, he cupped her behind again and pressed her against him so she could feel how he wanted her, how hard he was for her. He was so rigid, he ached.

She grabbed his shirt at his hips, pulling the fabric into tight fists. "I have a showing at six-thirty in the morning." After letting out a low groan of annoyance, she shook her head and leaned back to meet his eyes. "I need to be out of the house by six." She walked away while tucking an imaginary strand of hair behind her ear. "Ask me who's not a happy gal."

Those words sobered him up a bit, especially when Pete's case popped into his mind. "Where are you going?"

"Not far, just Dowfield." She began to clean up.

The image of her getting attacked didn't sit well. "Who's going with you?"

Oblivious to his thoughts, she casually stacked everything on the table into a single pile, laptop on the bottom. "No one, of course." Smoothly, she picked up the stack, and using her hip as support, she headed to her bedroom. "I'm meeting them there."

He watched her go but didn't follow. "Okay, then I'll go with you."

Quickly, she opened the door and, without going inside the room, she dumped her stack on the desk he had seen earlier. Closing the door again, she turned to him curiously and questioned, "Excuse me?" She tucked a couple of stray hairs behind her ear.

"Shae, don't you know what's going on in the area? Agents are getting attacked." He watched as she tilted her head in confusion, her brow frowning. He assumed her silence meant she didn't know, so he explained. "I met up with my old partner and he mentioned to me that real estate agents are getting assaulted. It's not safe, Shae. You should take one of your brothers with you."

"Excuse me?" She repeated as she crossed her arms.

Later, when he thought back to this moment, he would give himself a mental thrashing for not reading her correctly. The signs were all there, in her stance, in her voice. But he was so focused on keeping her safe, that he ignored them all.

It was his turn to frown. How could he explain it more clearly? "You can't go to showings by yourself."

Her lips pressed together, and though they raised in a semblance of a smile, there was a coolness to her eyes as they narrowed. "Listen, Jon, it's very sweet of you to care, but I've been doing this for a long time. I don't need anyone to hold my hand." The fake smile grew for a second when she finished saying, "But thank you for caring about my safety."

He imagined her going alone, early in the morning, and meeting up with an attacker. The image turned darker and he saw her face on one of those evidence pictures, her eyes open but unseeing, her pale skin completely devoid of color, her red lips turned blue. It was enough to churn his stomach. "No," he pushed. "You cannot do this alone. I will not allow it."

Shae's lips became a flat line and in a shrill voice, she said again, "Excuse me?!" Her pause didn't give him a chance to speak. Quickly, she demanded, "You did *not* just say that you—" she mocked his British accent and continued, "'—will not allow it,' did you?" She stepped closer to him, eyes blazing with rage. "No one—not even my own father—has the balls to tell me what I can and can't do."

Lena Lane

What the hell was her problem? Couldn't she see it? "You're in danger, damn it." He also stepped closer, their bodies so close, he could discern the different shades of pale blue in her eyes. They were lovely, even when she was raving mad. "I don't want you getting hurt, Shae. I care about you." There. That should help her understand. This wasn't about taking control of her or her life. This was about safety. He reached out and touched her face, gently caressing her cheek with his thumb, hoping the physical touch would convey how worried he was.

As he watched, she took a deep breath. He could see the struggle as she forced herself to relax. And when she spoke again, her voice barely shook as she tried to control her anger. "You know, my brother is also showing a property early in the morning. Will you be his bodyguard, too?"

Alarms rang through his mind. *Trick question! Trick question!* She asked knowing perfectly well that his answer would be no. That he didn't care about her siblings, only her. His hand dropped. How was he to explain this? If he actually said no, then she would take it as evidence that he thought her weak.

"Shae," he began, but she didn't allow him continue.

Outraged, she walked to the door and opened it. She stood there, by the door, stiff and straight, chin held high. "Thank you for stopping by, Mr. Rossi. I will reach out when I have confirmation on the appointments for the properties."

Mr. Rossi, eh? She was so angry with him that she didn't even want to use the familiarity of a first name. Internally, he shrugged. Fine. Whatever. She'll get over it. Eventually.

VICTORIAN SURPRISE

He grabbed his jacket and walked to the door. As they both stood there, the cool air of the November night brushing over them, he caressed the side of her cheek again, this time with the back of his hand. Her skin was as frigid as her attitude. He smiled and said simply, "Please be safe."

Stalking Behavior

It was his fault she was even *considering* being afraid. How many times had she done this? It was just another showing, at another property, with another couple of potential buyers. There was no reason to fear them.

Until Jon had brought up the ludicrous idea that she shouldn't show properties without another agent, there had never been any reason to be apprehensive about clients. They were just people looking for help.

Of course Sharon had heard the rumors of attacks. All agents had. That's what people do, they talk. Even her realtor association group had held a "Keeping It Safe" night. Police officers in the area presented some safety tips, and if needed, some self-defense instructions. There were plenty of recommendations for agents, one of which was to go out with others, as Jon said, but who had time for that? Time was a luxury no one in the real estate industry had.

Though right now, she wished she had listened to him.

Technically, there was no reason for Sharon to be uneasy. The two had introduced themselves as brothers looking to buy a duplex. They had been polite and easy going, had provided her with cell numbers that worked, and had a pre-approval letter with their name and current addresses. Everything had transpired like a thousand other initial meetings, so she hadn't thought twice about scheduling the showing.

VICTORIAN SURPRISE

And now, the three of them were wandering around the vacant property at six-thirty in the morning, with the sun barely cresting the horizon.

Perhaps it was the darkness that made her weary. Or maybe it was the conversation with Jon from the night before. But probably because the two brothers were always on either side of her, regardless of which room they were in, making her feel like a monkey-in-the-middle, being stalked from both sides.

Normal protocol was to invite the clients to go in first. Not only was it polite, it also gave agents a way out, if they ever needed to turn and run. But these guys insisted she lead. Rather than making it an issue, she conceded and led the way, which meant she had two big guys walking behind her. Once inside the property, they stood on either side of her. *Wonderful.* She made quick work of the showing, probably the fastest one she'd ever done. Soon enough, all three were outside in the backyard and she was breathing a sigh of relief.

By this time, the sun had colored the sky a beautiful blend of rose and lavender, the different shades sweeping across the horizon like a magnificent painting. And though she loved the colors nature had chosen, she hated being up so early. Still, she faked a smile and kept going.

"Well guys, that's it." Sharon looked from one to the other. "Do you have any questions?"

The two looked at each other and shared a nod. She knew a lot of communication had taken place with that single nod. She didn't know what it was, but it made her nervous again. At least they were outside now. With her hands deep in her pockets to keep her fingers warm, she held her two weapons: mace in one, keys in the other.

She could always stab one of them through the eye with a key if it came down to it.

The one closest to her spoke first, "Nope."

The other said, "Not right now. But we'll talk it over and call you later."

"Sounds like a plan, guys." She couldn't get away from them quickly enough. Walking back toward the house, she said, "Keep in touch."

She wasn't going to take any chances. Immediately upon entering the house again, she locked the door behind her. Once she was sure it was secure, she went through the house, turning off lights, making sure windows and the other doors were locked. Just as she was about to leave, she looked through the window to make sure the other car was gone. Noting that it was, she left.

And that's when she saw the *other* car. And it's driver.

Parked across the street, hiding behind some bushes and barren trees, Jon watched her through his open car window. Sharon stalked over, her anger mounting with each step, and as soon as she was within hearing distance, she demanded, "Did you follow me?" When he didn't answer within two seconds, she asked again, "Did. You. Follow. Me."

"Yes," he admitted, his dark eyes somber.

"That is not okay, Mr. Rossi." She was fuming. Her heart was threatening to beat out of her chest, and she was so angry, she wanted to punch him. Gripping the mace in her hand, she toyed with the idea of using it on him. "You worked for the police, correct? What type of behavior are you exhibiting, Mr. Rossi? Hm?" Rambling with an internal fire, she never gave him a chance to speak. "Because I'm thinking this falls under the category of stalking."

VICTORIAN SURPRISE

He tilted his head back a bit. "Come now, Shae."

"No, Jon. Following me is not okay." She shook her head, sending her hair all over her face. With angry swipes, she pushed it away, tucking it behind her ears with cold fingers. "I know you think you're trying to keep me safe, but it is never okay to go around and follow someone without their knowledge." She quickly added, "Or permission!"

"I know, alright?!" His voice rose in his defense. "Don't you think I know? I know. You don't need to remind me about stalking behavior, thanks." He shook his head and gripped the steering wheel tightly. Looking forward, he said, "I'll leave you be. I just wanted to make sure you were alright."

Without another word, she spun on her heels and headed to her car.

She's Gone

Bollocks! Jon could not believe he'd been caught. Had this been a stakeout with a suspect, he would have blown the entire operation. What had this woman done to him? Because, obviously, he was not thinking clearly. He shook his head in dismay at his own tactics. His old work mates would have a field day laughing at him. Not only could he *not* talk sense into the lady, he couldn't even keep an eye on her properly.

Though they didn't know how observant Miss Sharon Sampson was. Not much passed her keen eyes.

Jon watched Shae stalk away from him, stomping the concrete of the driveway with each step. He was surprised it didn't crack under the force of her rage. She was certainly pissed, but it was worth it to know she was alright. Since she wasn't there to see it, he allowed himself a little grin.

It faded quickly, though. Shae didn't need to remind him which law he had broken. There were actually quite a number of them, but he wasn't going to tell her. She didn't need any more fuel to be pissed at him. As he watched, she drove off in a huff, revving the engine, and leaving skid marks in her wake.

Turning his car around, he headed back to his apartment by driving in the opposite direction, all the while contemplating his next move.

Despite what she thought, she was an innocent with no true knowledge of how vulnerable she was to an attack. Jon thought back to the dinner she had with her family in Vegas. He had watched them for far too long, and they never noticed. And Sam may like to throw a punch or two to protect his family, but Jon doubted he had any true skill. Of course, that was better than Scott. As clean cut as he was, Jon doubted he could fight out of a wet paper bag. The trio may *believe* they knew how to keep each other safe; they had no idea.

Back in Vegas, he had toyed with the idea of giving them self-defense classes when the dojo was up and running. This just confirmed it. He would need to get this going sooner rather than later, and then invite them all.

Mind made up, he parked the car and went inside to have some breakfast.

And then a text came through that ruined his day; his month; his year.

Jon walked away from the stove when he read it, trying to process the words. They didn't register the first time. He had to read them a second, and third time, before they finally sank in. All thoughts of Shae and his dojo fled his mind. He went to the nearest chair and slumped into it, the weight of the words forcing him down. The butter on the frying pan continued to sizzle, waiting for eggs that never came.

She's gone.

Two words that shattered his world.

"Fuck..." It was spoken so softly that no one would have heard, even if he hadn't been alone. He put the phone on the table and leaned back, putting distance between him and the offending item. But it wasn't enough. In a fit of impotent frustration, he grabbed it and threw it across the room, where it hit the wall before landing on the tile floor with a shattered screen.

Lena Lane

With his elbows on the table, Jon closed his eyes and rested his forehead on the heels of his palms. The first tear he cried since he was fourteen, hit the table just as his phone dinged with another incoming text. He snorted. He didn't know if he was happy or sad that the phone still worked. But it didn't matter, because he had no intention of picking it up again. One painful message a day was enough.

The smell of smoke demanded his attention. He looked at the empty pan, still on the stove, and forced himself to take care of it before he set the place on fire. He'd forgotten all about it. After turning the heat off, he threw the pan into the sink. So much for breakfast.

An epiphany came to him then. *Liquid breakfast.*

Another first after a decade: he was drinking alone. Jon opened the bottle of scotch and poured himself a generous portion. He gulped it down in seconds, then poured himself another. After repeating it several times, he decided to be more efficient and no longer bothered with the glass. *Eh, who needs sobriety anyway?*

As he stumbled into the recliner in the living room, the bottle fell out of his hand. It landed with a thud by his feet. He looked at it, both offended and relieved. She would not be happy to see him like this.

It doesn't matter, she's gone anyway.

Broken hearted, he sobbed.

Another Agent

Sharon contemplated what she should do. If he didn't want to answer her texts or calls, it wasn't her problem. She had done what she'd said she'd do. She had scheduled showings for the three different locations, and had promptly texted him with the times.

And received no reply.

If he had been any other client, she would have just called the agents back and cancelled, and forgotten all about it.

But Jon wasn't just another client.

She still couldn't believe that he had followed her. No, she didn't regret saying what she had. Of course he couldn't go following her around —no matter the reason. It was creepy. She understood the need to protect those you cared about, and perhaps she should feel flattered that he cared about *her*, but he had gone too far.

Still, maybe she could have been kinder when saying so.

She had completely lost her cool when she saw him there, waiting for her, watching her. She'd been on edge already because of the buyers' behavior, insisting she go in first, flanking her as they walked through the property. Seeing Jon in his car just pushed her over.

It had been a long time since anyone had told her what to do. The last person who dared was her mother, and she'd been gone for almost four years. But even she would say Sharon blew up. There was a right way and a wrong way to communicate with people. And Sharon had gone overboard. She sighed. Perhaps she should go over to Jon's place and apologize. Not for what she'd said, but for how she'd said it.

With a sigh, she told herself she'd go in the morning.

Swaying World

The ringing was annoying the crap out of him.

Jon woke with a throbbing headache, his stomach threatening to empty, and when he stood, the world swayed. He gripped the armrest of the recliner, wondering if he'd truly had that much to drink. He sighed when he saw the confirmation still on the floor by his feet: the bottle of scotch, empty.

If that damn phone didn't stop ringing, he was going to break it in half.

Eventually the world stopped moving enough that he was able to get to the kitchen by using the walls for support. By the time he got there, though, the ringing had stopped. He picked up the phone and through the broken screen, he saw several texts and missed calls from Shae. The last text was a threat of cancellation for the three appointments she had scheduled for that day.

Cancelling was probably for the best, anyway. He had to head to New York for the next couple of weeks or so. Something he didn't want to think about, but he knew he had no choice.

He threw the phone onto the table and headed for a shower. He had to wash the cobwebs from his mind.

So Sorry

Sharon stood outside Jon's front door and looked at the doorbell. *Do I ring it? Do I not?* She bit her lower lip and swept her hair behind her ear while she tried to make up her mind. This decision should have been made long before she drove to his place, but why think something through when being impulsive worked most of the time? Sometimes? On occasion, for sure.

She squared her shoulders, raised her chin, and plastered her agent smile on her face. She raised her hand and pushed the button.

And waited.

And waited some more.

His car was parked out front, so she was pretty sure he was home.

Perhaps he wanted nothing to do with her anymore.

What the hell.

She pushed it again.

Seconds became minutes. And as the time passed, so did her patience.

What she was about to do was probably not the most professional thing she'd ever done, but he was pissing her off. She laid her finger on the buzzer and held it down. Jon could ignore her texts, maybe he had gone as far as to block her calls, but he couldn't ignore the buzzer forever. Her evil side beamed at the torture of continued buzzing echoing through the apartment. She imagined his dark eyes filled with anger that mirrored her own and grinned.

VICTORIAN SURPRISE

The door swung open to reveal Jon, covered in water and not much else. "Bloody fuckin' hell."

Oh yes, he was fuming all right. But she had stopped looking at his face.

Instead, her gaze followed droplets of water as they ran down his neck, onto his chest. She wanted to run her hands over it, wanted to rub her palms on his wet nipples. Then she followed other droplets that ran further, over hard abs and onto that natural dip at his hips that made her lose her mind. All logical thought fled as she saw him in his naked glory.

"Why are you here, Shae?" Jon demanded.

Immediately, her eyes locked with his. The words were a bit of a shock, considering what was going through her mind. Wasn't he a detective in his previous work life? She was pretty sure he should know why she was there.

"Why do you think?!" The sarcasm was thick when she continued, "I'm here for a lay. Maybe suck your cock?" The words came out unexpectedly. But once they were out, she admitted to herself that she'd like that, very much. Sure, she was there for different reasons, but would it be horrible if she took a bit of a side trip? Damn, but he had an incredible way of sending all logical thought from her mind.

While she stared at his face, she watched his anger diminish. Not all of it, but enough. He backed up and allowed her to step inside, then closed the door behind her. Without a word, he walked through a door immediately off the living room. Following him into his bedroom, she watched him head for an armchair where he picked up clothes and threw them carelessly to the floor, then sat with his cock growing in expectation of attention. He sat there like a king, hands on the armrests, and waited.

Sharon shrugged off her jacket and threw it on the bed, along with her bag. Without preamble, she knelt in front of him and took him deep into her mouth. He tasted clean. Delicious.

The water from his shower still covered his body; it was cold to the touch. She ran her hands over his legs, collecting droplets as she went, while licking his shaft, base to tip. With her nails, she scraped his thighs lightly as she brought her hands closer and closer to it. When she got there, she gripped him tightly, and held him as she ran her tongue across the tip. Fluid was pooling there, not water from his shower, but something that was uniquely his. She licked it up, savoring the taste, savoring him.

She watched as his eyes became heavy, and eventually closed altogether, the sensations drawing moans of pleasure from him. So erotic. She loved every sound. Wanting more, she gripped him tightly and licked and sucked and gently bit him. She heard his groans, heard his sharp intake of breath, and knew he was loving it.

When she leaned back to reposition herself, he grabbed her head and pulled her forward. He shoved himself into her mouth so hard, so deep, she thought she might gag. Sharon laughed. Forcing him to release her, she shook her head, and she said, "Nah. I'm in charge."

He took that as a challenge, because he grinned and asked, "You think so?"

Without giving her an opportunity to respond, he stood. The next thing she knew, she was on her back, on the bedroom rug, her skirt hiked up to her hips, and her panties stuck on the heel of her boot. After covering himself up with a condom he grabbed from his wallet, he pounded into her, hard and fast. She barely had time to breathe. It didn't take her long to shatter around him. Arching her back, she held onto his shoulders and wrapped her legs around his hips, pulling him deep into her so she could hold him as she climaxed.

He shuddered with his own release, then collapsed on the floor beside her. A moment later, he was removing the used condom.

After her breathing and her pounding heart returned to normal, she broke the silence. "Well, you showed me."

He didn't find it amusing. Or he didn't care. "Why are you here, Shae?"

She took a deep breath and focused on the ceiling. Looking at the light above them, she said, "You didn't answer me."

She felt his eyes on her. "Do you mean your calls and texts?"

"Yes."

He looked up to study the ceiling as well. "I was indisposed."

Sharon didn't know what that meant. And she wasn't sure she wanted to know. Indisposed with something else? Indisposed with *someone* else? "What does that mean?"

"It means I was busy." He got up and looked down at her. "It means I don't have time for you right now." He turned and threw the used condom in the trash, the move almost violent.

She was shocked. She would have thought that after a blow and a fuck, he would have relaxed some, but no. Well, she'd had enough of his nasty attitude. "Why are you being such a dick? What happened to the man I met on the plane? What happened to the man I spent time with in Vegas?"

"That man had been on holiday. He didn't have a care in the world." He crossed his arms and looked down his nose at her. "This one does."

"Well," Sharon sat up and tried to grab her panties from the heel of her boot. "I'm very sorry," she tugged so hard, they tore, "that I bothered you." She stood up and flung them into the trash with as much force as he had thrown the condom. "But if you remember," she straightened her skirt down, "*you* were the one who came to *me* for help." She looked around the room, searching for her jacket and bag. Angrily, she picked up the jacket and shook it. "As a client who had shown some urgency in finding the perfect place," she turned and finally met his gaze, "I thought that something might've been wrong when you didn't reply." She shoved an arm into the jacket, then the other. "When you're ready to move forward," she grabbed her bag, "find another agent." Furiously, she stalked through the living room to the front door, flung it wide, and spat over her shoulder, "Have a terrible day." She slammed the door shut behind her.

As she walked to her car, she tried to ignore the delicious tingling that her clit still felt, the echoes of an amazing climax. She was too mad at him to give him credit for being the best lover she'd ever had.

Then again, if this was their last time together, she might want to commit it to memory. Because, *Damn, he was good.*

Mama Mabel

Jon considered calling Shae, maybe texting her. Hell, he could have sent her a postcard from New York. But he hadn't. Because doing so would be admitting he'd been an asshole. And right now, he was too busy burying the only mother he'd ever known. Shae would have to wait until his return for an apology.

From the doorway, he looked at the room full of people he'd known as a kid, most of whom he had called family even though there was no biological connection. His gaze landed briefly on the line of four men closest to the casket, his *brothers*—Jon used the term loosely—dressed in their Sunday best. After everything that passed in his childhood, he wished he'd never met them. But like it or not, they were the closest thing to family she'd had, and they were all her children—even if not biological. It was a package deal.

Mama Mabel, as they called her, had tried to convince the five boys that it would be better to be nice to each other, to help each other, to treat one another as family, rather than to be adversaries. What she'd forgotten was that the boys' biological families were all trash. So, yes, they did treat one another like family: they threatened each other, stole from each other, and on occasions, they'd beat each other up. Because that's all they knew of *family*.

Jon had been the last to arrive at Mama Mabel's house. By then, she already had the four others. Barry had been the youngest at seven. Then there was Billy, ten; Frank, eleven; and the eldest, Terry, was fifteen. Jon had been nine when he first walked through that door. By that time, though, Jon had learned a lot of lessons, including how to take a punch. So when the four came to *welcome* him, he hadn't even flinched.

Jon hadn't been back since he'd left on his eighteenth birthday, choosing to keep in touch with Mama by phone. Billy was the only one he had bothered to text on occasion, just so he could know the truth about what was going on with Mama. At this point, though, Jon wasn't sure if there would be any further texts. The only reason for their contact was now gone.

His mind drifted to Shae. What had her childhood been like, he wondered. Considering her overprotective brothers, probably full of love and support. Jon imagined a house in the suburbs, with a white picket fence, and a pet, probably a dog. It was the kind of place he had dreamt of as a kid, with a mom who was around to kiss his scrapes, and a dad who wanted to spend time with him—sober. Of course, that had been decades ago. And that dream had faded into oblivion before he'd hit his teens.

As he walked back to his spot by the casket, he was reminded of his own mortality. Mama Mabel had been his one and only true parent. The only one who cared if he ate and was well, the only one who bothered to take him to the doctors if he was sick. If he were to die—right then and there—no one in the room would care. They'd probably throw his body into a dumpster and forget he ever existed.

Luckily, he still had Aly. But she had her own battles to fight.

Would Shae care?

VICTORIAN SURPRISE

Interrupting his thoughts, Barry leaned over to Jon and whispered, "When do you want to go through the stuff at the house?"

Never, Jon wanted to say. Of all the things he wanted to do, go through his dead mother's things was not one of them. Out loud, he said, "Let's talk about it tomorrow."

He had no idea why he'd been selected as executor of Mama's estate. He wanted no part of it. But no sooner had he walked in the house than the papers were shoved in his hand. The others had asked him to read them immediately, but he couldn't bring himself to do it. Jon made up an excuse, saying was too tired at the time. Then he'd made up other excuses about being busy with funeral arrangements. Technically, everything he'd said was true, but if he'd really wanted to, he would have read them sooner. He just wasn't ready. He needed time to process it all.

The more the others nagged him, the longer he wanted to wait. Bastards wanted to make money from her death. They knew they were her only family, too, and they expected everything to go to them. Wouldn't it be a kick in the balls if she left her money to charity? All of a sudden it hit him that she might very well have done just that. For the first time since he received the text, he smiled.

It's Over

Each time her phone dinged or rang, Sharon looked at it quickly, then sighed with disappointment when it wasn't from the person she was missing. She had no idea what had happened, but something had gone seriously wrong. She only wished she knew what.

Since her impromptu trip to Jon's place, she'd gone back to work and forgotten all about him. *Or tried to,* her mind corrected quickly. *Shut it, Shae,* she told herself, *you have way too much to do to waste time thinking about someone who obviously doesn't care about you.*

After everything that had happened between them, after she shared so much with him and he'd been so supportive and understanding, she thought they would be open with each other. *Guess not.* She might have opened up to him, but he wanted to keep his secrets. And now, he wanted to keep his distance. Fine. Screw him.

Sharon's life had reverted back to the constant running around that had driven her almost mad. With the others back, things were a bit more manageable, but not by much. *So much for a mini vacation to reset.* It was as if that trip to Vegas had never happened. A void in time; a dream. If it wasn't for how much she missed Jon, she would think she imagined the whole thing.

It was close to two weeks and she hadn't heard a word from him: no call, no text. She had contemplated calling or texting him herself, but considering the circumstances she left his place in the last time they

VICTORIAN SURPRISE

were together, she couldn't bring herself to do it. Perhaps her momentary escape from reality had come to its inevitable end. It would be ironic. After all, she was the one who said she wanted an escape *for a time*; she was only looking for *temporary* fun. It seemed it was over.

Now, it was back to reality.

Choke Hold

The four of them were staring at Jon as if he'd lost his mind. Jon, on the other hand, was trying to contain his amusement, but it was incredibly difficult. *Oh, Mama, I'm going to miss you.*

"What do you mean 'get a job?'" Terry voiced the question the others were thinking. The burly jerk was leaning over the armrest of the recliner, his brow furrowed as he attempted to resolve the difficult puzzle.

"It's very simple," Jon tried again. "Once you show evidence of a tax return with a net income of fifteen thousand dollars, at minimum, you'll be able to receive your inheritance." He looked over at the other three and cleared his throat, faking a brief coughing spasm to cover the laughter he was suppressing. They stared blankly at him with wide eyes and slack jaws, their mouths gaped open. If he had a bowl of nuts, he'd be throwing them, one at a time, into the openings and counting points.

"What kinda job?" Barry was just as lost and confused as the others. He scratched his balding head and moved the few strands he had left back.

"It doesn't matter," Jon replied. "As long as it's legal, you report it to the IRS, and you pay your taxes, you'll be fine."

"But fifteen thousand is a lot of money." It was Frank's turn to voice his worries. He was just sitting on edge of the couch, clutching his hands and shaking his head. "How much time do we have to come up with it again?"

The amusement was fading fast, and rapidly being replaced by annoyance at their ignorance. "A year, Frank." Jon passed his hand over his face in frustration. "You can make this money by working a minimum wage job for a year."

"You're lying!" Terry suddenly flew up from his chair in a huff, shoving it angrily out of his way and scratching Mama's ancient wood floor. He advanced threateningly and didn't stop until he was almost in Jon's face.

Remaining calm, Jon held the papers up, offering them to Terry. "Feel free to read it yourself." Looking at the others in the room, he went on, "You should all read it."

Barry showed some progress in understanding with his next question. "But if we won't get the money for a year, how are we supposed to live here?" He looked at the others in the room. "I mean, how we gonna get money for food?"

"Well, Barry," Jon answered patiently, and tried his best not to be condescending. It was quite the challenge. "Mama will take care of paying the bills for a year and a half. That gives you six months to find a job."

"How the fuck is she gonna do that?" Billy finally spoke from his place by the window. "She's dead."

"She asked me to take care of it on her behalf," Jon clarified.

"Yeah?" It was Terry who questioned. "Sounds to me like you're gonna get our cash." He looked around the room at the others. "And we're supposed to trust him? Trust that he'll do right by us?" He strode closer and closer to where Jon sat, his anger reflected in his beady eyes. "Trust you with *our* money?" He looked down at Jon, hovering over him with his hands curled into fists.

Jon sighed and stood up. He might miss Mama, but he certainly didn't miss these assholes. "Like it or not, mate, that's how it's going to be."

"I ain't your mate." Terry pushed at Jon's chest, trying to knock him back down onto the couch.

It didn't work.

Barely swaying, Jon felt his body react to the threat. His heart beat a little faster, his gaze became a bit sharper. He was acutely aware of Terry's distance, his stance, even his breathing. In preparation for the oncoming fight, Jon let the papers fall on the chair behind him and raised his hands between them in a passive gesture. "I don't want to fight, Terry. I just came here to help."

"I don't think that's true, Jonathan." Terry emphasized his name. "I think you came here to steal from us and you think we're too stupid to realize it."

"Well, Terrance," Jon mocked him, "though I agree that you are too stupid to understand much of anything, I'm not here to steal your money." He had plenty of time to sidestep in order to avoid the incoming fist. "See? You've just confirmed your own stupidity." Another sidestep in the other direction, the punch so far off, Terry swayed and almost fell over on his own. "Do you have any idea what I've been doing for the past decade?"

"I don't know, Jonathan," Terry mocked again, this time with a fake British accent, "maybe having tea and crackers with the Queen?"

VICTORIAN SURPRISE

As Terry swung for the third time, Jon hit his elbow and used the momentum to push him farther until his back was against Jon's front. *And here I was, thinking my accent was fading.* Trapping him, Jon held his head in a choke hold. "The saying is 'tea and crumpets,' Terry." He continued to hold fast while Terry struggled to break free. "I should thank you, you know. All of you." Jon ignored the slaps to his arms and head, ignored the scratches at his face. "Because of you, and dear old dad of course, I found out I was really good at fighting. So good, in fact, that I was able to get my sixth degree black belt." Jon could feel Terry's body losing energy; his slaps were weaker, his weight heavier. "I made quite a bit o' money fighting." Once Terry's body became limp with unconsciousness, Jon let it fall to the floor and stepped back. It wasn't a gentle drop. "I can assure you, I don't need yours."

When Terry's body landed, three sets of wide eyes landed on Jon. They hadn't moved, but simply watched with morbid curiosity. He suspected that they couldn't believe their leader had been taken down. No one challenged Terry. At least not when they were kids. He doubted things had changed in his absence.

"Well," Jon said to the others, "if you've no other questions, I think I'll head home now." He gave them a few seconds to respond, but when no one spoke, he grabbed his jacket and left.

Merry Christmas

Sampson Realty was decorated for the holidays. On the door was a wreath with berries, pine cones, and a bright red ribbon. On the floor-to-ceiling windows, painted snowflakes gave the office a cheery look, while inside, a small tree stood in the corner, twinkling with happy lights.

Not that Sharon noticed any of this as she walked past the reception counter. Barely greeting the new receptionist they had finally hired, she made her way to her office and began to shrug off her winter coat. She looked past the small group of bright envelopes containing well wishes for the season and focused on her calendar. Then swore. Shrugging the coat back on, she grabbed her bag and headed back out. Other folks may be enjoying their holiday season, but she had too much to do, which included getting the fire certificate for her next closing. Something she should have gotten a week ago.

Driving a little faster than the law allowed, she made it to the fire department just in time. She plastered a smile on her face and walked calmly to the counter where Anna was waiting and shaking her head.

"Hi, Sharon," she greeted with a grin, "cutting it close, aren't you?" Anna reached under the counter and pulled out an envelope.

"Anna, honey, how are you?" Ignoring the question, Sharon rested her chin on the heel of her hand and leaned on the counter as if she had not a care in the

VICTORIAN SURPRISE

world. With her other hand, she reached into her pocket and pulled out the check she needed to pay for the certificate. Sliding the check across the counter, she asked, "Ready for Christmas?"

"Yes, I'm so excited!" Anna took the check and processed it.

With pleasantries done and the certificate in hand, Sharon should leave, but Anna's chocolate brown eyes were bright with joy. Something exciting was going on; she had to know more. "I haven't seen you like this since you first got this job." Giving her a sideways look, Sharon asked, "What's going on?"

Anna didn't hesitate. "Dave and I are going away for New Years!" She put the check and log away, then leaned on the counter, too. "This past year has been incredible. He is so amazing. Sweet, gentle, kind."

"That's Dave." Faking a similar joyful expression, Sharon grinned and grabbed Anna's hands to give them a gentle squeeze. "I'm so happy for you."

"And it's all thanks to you." Anna's voice broke with emotion, her eyes welling up a bit. "If you hadn't sent me to drop those papers at his office, I never would have met him." It was her turn to give Sharon's hands a squeeze. "What luck."

"Yes..." Sharon had known immediately that Anna would be a far better match for her cousin than the woman he was trying to date, Sarah. By that time, Sarah and Scott were too far gone into each other to have someone like Dave step in.

Seems like everything ended well, though. For everyone except *her*. Sharon had to give herself a mental shake. *Knock it off.* To Anna, she said, "I'm very happy for you two. Have a wonderful Christmas and New

Year's." Sharon grabbed the certificate off the counter, then gave her friend a wave as she left.

The frigid air of winter bit her face as soon as she was outside. As she walked back to her car, a wave of sadness came over her. She should be happy for them, but as she thought about everyone around her, happily paired off, she was far from happy. She was still a solitary pigeon no one wanted. Maybe she should get a cat. She tried to laugh, but the sound was too close to a sob to contain any humor.

Driving back to her office, she let her mind wander.

Six weeks and counting. That's how long it's been since she'd last seen Jon. Not that she was missing him any. After all, *she* was the one who told him to get going. He'd been acting like a jerk, and worse, weird and stalker-like. She didn't need someone like him in her life.

Though she might, if he behaved like he did when they'd first met.

Actually, he was an odd duck when you first met, remember?

She thought back to that first encounter at the airport and laughed. Yeah, he was an odd duck. But after that, he had been charming, funny, and understanding. For the first time in a long time, Sharon was able to be herself. That escape in Vegas had been perfect, and she'd remember it forever.

But now, she was back to being Sharon Sampson, the real estate agent. With a deep sigh of regret at her unchanged circumstances, she got in her car and headed back.

After she parked her car, she was walking back to her office with hands deep in her pockets when her phone began to ring. *Forget it.* She wasn't going to pull her hands from her cozy pockets to answer it. Whoever

VICTORIAN SURPRISE

it was could wait until she was back in her office, and her blood began to flow through her frozen fingers again. It was only half a minute away, anyway. She continued walking and ignored the ding of the incoming voicemail. That could wait, too.

Old Victorian

Jon left the voicemail but wasn't sure if Shae would actually call him back. Considering the tone of their last encounter, he wouldn't be surprised if she didn't. Still, one could hope.

The trip had taken far longer than he'd expected. He'd thought the whole thing would have been wrapped up in no more than a couple of weeks, but he'd been wrong. A month later, he'd still been working to get everything, including his so-called-brothers, in order. Only after grueling six weeks, had he been able to leave there.

He still hadn't apologized.

Jon hoped Shae would understand that it was important to him apologize in person.

After sorting out the situation in New York, he'd come back and resumed his search for potential properties on his own. One particular property caught his interest, and he really hoped it would work out. He didn't need her to go see it with him, but the truth was, he wanted her there. He missed Shae. Missed her boldness, her humor, her smile. Somehow, she was a blend of strength and vulnerability. It was an intoxicating combination.

Parking his car outside the place, an old Victorian in the center of the city, Jon turned up the heater and went over the description and pictures on his cell phone. According to them, the first floor was mostly open, perfect for a dojo, with an office in the back for the

VICTORIAN SURPRISE

thrilling paperwork. The remainder of the house was a living space. It would be perfect for him. At least it appeared to be.

Jon was about to drive off when his phone rang. A shot of excitement ran through him when he saw her name show up on his phone. "Hello, Shae."

"Did you think I wouldn't recognize who you were?" Not the greeting he'd hoped for, but still, he was happy she called him back at all. "I do know your name is Jonathan."

"Of course, love," he assured her. "But I'm calling on business and wanted to be a tad more formal."

"Right." She stretched the i sound in the word, making it known that she didn't believe him. "If you say so." But the sarcasm in her voice dropped minimally when she said, "Don't forget, I know your voice."

Perhaps it was unkind, but he hoped his voice haunted her as much as hers haunted him, especially at night when he lay in bed waiting for sleep, remembering their time together in Vegas and wishing she was with him. "As I know yours."

Seconds passed without a response, and he imagined her biting the lips he so loved to kiss. Maybe she was reminiscing, as well.

"Regardless," she said sharply into the silence, "what can I do for you?"

Bollocks. "There is a property I'd like to see. I'm hoping you can schedule a time."

He heard her sigh. Softly, she said, "I don't think this is a good idea, Jon." Before he was able to challenge her comment, she continued, "There are a lot of good agents out there. Someone else can help you."

"Oh, come now, Shae," he argued, "I don't want to have to explain everything to a new person, not when you already know everything." He exaggerated his own sigh. "I'd so dislike wasting time having to repeat everything to someone else." When her reply wasn't forthcoming, he pressed, "I promise I'll be good."

A heartbeat later, she said, "Fine, I'll send my brother. What's the address?"

Bollocks! His lackluster response would no doubt tell her his thoughts on this idea, but still, he gave her the address.

"I'll text the appointment time." Abruptly, she ended the call.

If she thought that the lack of pleasantries or a formal goodbye would bother him, she was sadly mistaken. If anything, it told him she felt *something*. The opposite of love wasn't hate. It was indifference. And she was far from being numb to him.

Jon drove home with a grin on his face.

Scheduled Showing

Sharon gave herself an extra fifteen minutes before the showing would begin, plenty of time to unlock doors and turn all lights on before the scheduled meeting time.

Try as she might, she couldn't convince either Scott or Sarah to take on another appointment, so she had to see it through. Maybe one of them would have, if she had explained that the buyer was Jon, the guy from Vegas, but she wasn't going to admit that she didn't want to see him. They would demand details she wasn't prepared to share.

Besides, she was a professional. She had plenty of experience with awkward situations. This was just another one to see through.

Apparently, however, fifteen minutes wasn't enough time to be *early*. When she arrived, there was another car already parked in the lot. She sighed in dismay and shook her head. *Whatever.* Parking her car next to his, she scowled and looked around for him. Since the house was vacant and still locked, he must be in the backyard.

Sharon got out of the car and walked to the front door thinking that she would let him walk around outside if he wanted to. She let herself in using the key in the lockbox and proceeded to open the place up.

Looking around, her immediate thought was that it would be good for him. It was in a mixed zone location, and the first floor was previously used as a storefront.

Lena Lane

Empty now, there was plenty of open space in the front, and a small room in the back that could be used for storage or an office.

The two upper floors were being used as a residential rental. There was nothing spectacular about the setup. The first floor of the unit contained the living room, kitchen, dining area, and a half bath. Upstairs were two bedrooms and a full bath. At least, they were spacious, if filthy. But nothing a good cleaning couldn't fix.

It didn't take long. In five minutes, everything was on and open, and Sharon headed back downstairs to look for her client. It was strange to think of Jon as a *client*, especially after everything they'd done together. But if he could get past it, so could she.

Sharon went down the two flights of stairs and was walking to the front door when someone outside caught her attention. *There he is.* She walked over to the window with the intention of calling for him, but froze when she realized it wasn't Jon, but someone else. After opening the window, she called out, "Excuse me?"

The stranger looked up and locked eyes with her. "Hello, there."

Not an agent, and not the owner, Sharon didn't know who he was, but he was dressed in a sharp, leather jacket and pressed slacks. A little older, and a little rounder in the middle, he had impeccable taste in clothing. Perhaps another buyer, or an investor. "May I help you?"

"Maybe." He motioned to the building and the surrounding land. "I'm interested in acquiring the property. Are you the owner?"

"No," she replied, "I'm a real estate agent. I have—"

A firm hand clamped her mouth shut while another wrapped around her midriff and dragged her back.

VICTORIAN SURPRISE

Stumbling, she fell onto a hard body standing behind her. Immediately, she tried to free herself, pulling and scratching at any skin her nails could get. She squirmed, twisted, and struggled within the masculine limbs, fighting the hold, but the strong body behind her simply lifted her off the floor. She no longer had the leverage of solid footing.

At the moment, she could think of nothing more than her freedom. Her fear was bordering on panic, but she refused to freeze and become another statistic. Thankful for her heels, she kicked straight back, hoping to hit something. Luck was not on her side. Her reward for trying was a grunt and a curse, followed by an even tighter hold around her middle, so tight her stomach ached. Weakened from the exertion and lack of air, she gave up. For the time being.

Once they were in the small room in back of the retail space, he let her go. At the sudden release, she dropped to the floor, hitting her hip on the hard concrete. Pain shot through her, radiating up her lower back and down her legs. She pushed up and supported her upper body with both hands, legs resting on the cold floor, and looked at him over her shoulder. To her surprise, he was not alone.

"Aren't you a cutie?" The stranger from outside stood in the doorway looking down at her.

Trying not to lose herself in the situation, she said, "Thank you. It takes hours of hard work." His coarse laughter sent shivers down her spine. *Stay calm. Keep a clear head. You won't be alone for long.* If she kept him talking, maybe Jon would show up and rescue her. He was a former detective, and a fighter. Pulling at strings, she commented on the first thing that had left an impression. "I love your jacket. Very stylish."

"I'm glad you like it." He tugged at it and turned a little sideways so she could see more. "I got it in Italy. Paid a pretty price for it, but it's worth it."

"A good designer is always worth the cost." Flinching with pain, she repositioned herself to sit on her butt so the pressure against her hip would alleviate a bit. It didn't help. Keeping herself up with both hands behind her, she asked, "What's next?"

His smile was cold and calculating. "What do you think about having some fun?"

Sharon laughed and hoped it didn't sound panicked. Instead of replying, she swept her hair away from her face and looked at them, really looked at them, and her stomach dropped at what she saw in their eyes. She forced herself to stay focused. If nothing else, she would have a good description for the cops.

The Suit, as she was now mentally referring to him, was a little under six feet, had dark hair and dark eyes, a round, pudgy nose, and thin lips, and the orange skin of someone who'd been in a tanning booth. As she zeroed in on his face, she noticed a scar on his cheek and another on the side of his throat. Considering he was the one talking, he was probably the brains of the team.

The Muscle was younger, probably around her age, wearing a t-shirt and jeans. With similar features, they could be related, but she wasn't about to ask for confirmation. He'd almost be cute if he hadn't assailed her, dropped her on the concrete floor—possibly breaking her hip—and had clear intentions of other assaults.

The Suit's patience fled on her lack of a response. "You know, cutie, it's a lot more fun if you try to run." He took his jacket off.

VICTORIAN SURPRISE

A nervous giggle escaped, so she bit her lips to keep quiet. After taking a calming breath, she said, "I hate to disappoint, honey, but I think my hip might be broken. Running is not an option right now."

"That's too bad." Carefully, he shook the jacket and looked around. Not finding a suitable place for the extravagant piece, he handed it to Muscle, who took it without comment.

"Would it help if I scream?" *Gotta keep him talking. Just long enough for Jon to get here.*

"No," He shook his head and unbuttoned his slacks. "I don't want the neighbors to hear and interrupt us."

"Of course. That would be very disappointing." *Damn it, Jon, where are you?!*

Bloody Concrete

Jon was surprised to see two cars parked in the lot when he arrived, doubly so when one of them was Shae's. She had been quite firm about not wanting to be here; what could have changed her mind? Whatever it was, he was glad he'd be able to see her. He still owed her an apology.

Heading to the front door, he passed both cars and noticed the first had an out-of-state plate. His pace slowed. That car didn't belong to another agent in the area, certainly not anyone in her family. Who was with her? Could she have scheduled another showing at the same time? His gut told him no.

Thinking back to his conversation with Pete, his stomach dropped. He wanted to run inside and find her, make sure she was all right, but he was too well trained to do anything so rash. He needed to slow down and think things through. Cautiously, he stalked around the building, looking into windows, getting as many details on the layout as he could.

When he got to the back door, he saw them, two assholes standing in a doorway to a room not far from where he stood. From this angle, he was able to see Shae on the floor, on her side, propping herself up. When she moved to sit, she winced.

Immediately, he wanted a gun and some bullets. He wanted to charge in there and finish them. He had to remind himself that he no longer carried a weapon. And considering what he wanted to do, that was a good thing.

Quietly, he tried the nob and prayed that it would turn, then sent a mental thanks to Sharon for unlocking the doors. He opened it just an inch, afraid that it'd squeak if it went any further, and listened.

"You know, cutie, it's a lot more fun if you try to run."

Jon didn't know which asshole commented, but it was enough to boil his blood. Once he knew Shae was safe, he was going to skin this man alive. He heard her nervous giggle and pushed the door farther. Thankfully, it remained silent.

"I hate to disappoint, honey, but I think my hip might be broken. Running is not an option right now."

Fuck! Jon pulled his cell from his pocket and called 911. After lowering the volume all the way down, he put it on a windowsill so emergency personnel would be able to hear everything going on, and these guys wouldn't know. They'd also trace the call. Hopefully, this area still had a better response time than some others.

"That's too bad."

Squeak or no squeak, he couldn't leave her alone anymore. He pushed the door open enough that he could sneak inside.

"Would it help if I scream?"

Jon couldn't help himself; he smiled. Even in such a dire situation, with a potentially broken hip, she was still sassy. He couldn't wait to kiss her.

"No, I don't want the neighbors to hear and interrupt us."

"Of course. That would be very disappointing."

Lena Lane

Glad that he wore his sneakers, he was able to surprise the three of them. He began with the older one. Grabbing him by the scuff of his shirt, Jon threw him toward the open storefront and enjoyed watching the bastard slide on the concrete. *That's going to leave a mark.* He sensed, more than saw, the incoming fist and ducked just in time. He avoided getting punched by the younger one easily enough. Using the momentum of pulling back on the right, Jon followed up with an uppercut to the bastard's chin, sending him flying. When he landed, he didn't get back up. *One down.*

As much as he wanted to check on Shae, he couldn't until he knew *both* of them were out of commission. Though he would prefer dead, unconscious was a suitable option for now.

The older one stood back up. With a vicious growl, he tried to make a run at Jon, but struggled with his open pants. They were sliding down around his hips and he struggled to hold them up while weaving wildly toward Jon.

Understanding of the bastard's intent came quickly. So did Jon's rage. Without wasting another minute, Jon ran at him and began punching. Jab, cross, hook, uppercut, all in quick succession. There was no need to think about it. After so many years of training, muscle memory took over. A knee to the face, a sweep of the legs. And when he went down, Jon followed, straddling him and striking until blood stained the floor.

"Jon, stop!" The voice came from a distance. "Please! Jon! Stop it!"

Soft taps were landing on his shoulder, but he didn't care. Whoever it was couldn't stop him. Nothing would stop him until this bastard was dead.

"Damn it! Jon!"

VICTORIAN SURPRISE

All of a sudden, Shae's face was in front of his own, her tiny hand wrapped around his wrist. Still in motion, her hold didn't even slow him down. The momentum pulled her until she landed on the floor, right next to the bastard, her face in the pool of his blood. Seeing her there woke him from his rage. Immediately, he went to her.

Kneeling beside her, he cried, "Oh my God, Shae." Jon shifted and sat on the floor before lifting her head and gently placing it on his lap.

"For the love of all that is holy, Jonathan Rossi!" she yelled at him while pushing her hair from her face. The move spread the red streaks across her cheek and forehead. "Are you done yet?"

"Yes, God, yes."

"Took you long enough to get here," she snorted. Looking down at her watch, she complained, "Our appointment was at ten o'clock, not ten-fifteen."

He knew she didn't want him to know, but he could see the pain on her face, could see her other hand still pressing against her hip. Unwilling to see the red smudges on her face any longer, he took his shirt off and used it to wipe them off.

"Hey, I was here—on time." Jon played along knowing she needed some distraction from what had happened. Playing it down, he turned the experience into a joke. "But you decided to get knocked around by two thugs." Gently, he cleaned her face and hands. He wanted her porcelain skin perfect again.

"Well, I was getting bored waiting for yo—"

"Police! Everybody freeze!"

Impotent Rage

"You're lucky, Jonny," Pete said coming into the room and closing the door behind him. "I don't think you would have walked away from this if you didn't have such a good reputation in the department."

Jon looked at his old partner and said, "You know what he would've done if I hadn't stopped him." He'd been sitting in the interrogation room for far too long with nothing but a cup of nasty coffee to drink, and his patience was wearing thin.

"The problem isn't that you stopped him and you know it." Pete sat across from him. "The problem is the *enthusiasm* you did it with, if you catch my drift." He spun his chair so he was sitting facing the door, but rested his arm on the table, pretending to be relaxed. "Intent or not, he never touched her."

Well aware of the tactics he himself had used at one time, Jon took a deep breath and played the game. "As I mentioned before, Detective Leveque," he then proceeded to echo the official statement he'd already made to the officers, "I walked in on the two of them about to assault Ms. Sampson. The man wearing the suit had unbuttoned—"

"Jonny, come on," Pete interrupted him with a tap on the table.

"—his slacks. I overheard Ms. Sampson comment that she believed her hip was broken."

"Alright, alright." Pete's exasperated voice broke in again. He signed and scratched his balding head. "You are one smart bastard and you know how to play the system. We won't get anywhere until you tell us what really happened."

Annoyed and insulted, Jon shook his head. He scowled at his old friend. "I'm not playing the system, Detective Leveque. I walked in on a woman being attacked, and I put a stop to it."

"Don't give me that shit, Jonny. There were a thousand ways you could have done that without beating the fuck out of him. Let's see," he lifted his hand and began counting on his fingers, "one broken nose, two black eyes, a chipped tooth, two broken ribs, countless lacerations." He spun in the chair to face Jon head-on. "Do you know how many stitches he needed?"

Jon didn't much care. Whatever he got, he deserved. Bitterly, he challenged, "One for each assault he committed?"

"That's not your job!" Pete yelled back while slamming his hand against the table. Pointing at Jon, he pushed, "You are *not* judge and executioner." Frustrated, he threw his hands in the air. "You're not even on the force anymore. You should have called 911 and walked away."

"And let him go through with his plans? Sit back and watch him rape Shae?" It was Jon's turn to slam his hand on the table. In a fit of impotent rage, he stood up quickly, sending his chair flying backward. "Fuck him and fuck you." It landed with a loud thud, a stark sound in an otherwise silent room.

"Admit it, Jonny," Pete pushed, "this is personal and you know it."

Realizing that he was being bated, Jon let out a bitter laugh. He had to remember his training. *Breathe.* He took a deep breath while he picked up his chair. Calmly sitting down, he began to recite his statement, "I walked in on the two of them about to assault Ms. Sampson. The man wearing the suit had unbuttoned—"

Pete walked out.

Moving On

"I'm fine!" If Sharon had to say that—even one more time—she was going to explode. Maybe she should make a recording, and play it each time someone told her she should be home, resting.

"But you were just—" Sarah was being nice and supportive. It was sweet that she cared.

But Sharon was having none of it. "Shut it!" She bit out. Immediately, she ran a hand over her face in regret. "I'm sorry, Sarah. But you'll just have to trust me. I'm okay. I promise."

Without waiting for a response, Sharon left her sister-in-law by the reception area and returned to her office after grabbing the listings from the printer. She went back to business.

Although her hip still ached, the hospital had told her it wasn't broken, and the pain would subside in a few days. That was three days ago. Until it passed, she could take some over-the-counter medicine, if needed. But she didn't. Because it wasn't broken and she could deal with it.

What *had* become a pain was her family, constantly nagging her and asking if she were all right. That had been *her* mistake. She had needed a ride back from the hospital and she couldn't find Jon. Eventually breaking down, she had called the "quiet one," Sammy, hoping he would keep things to himself. If she knew then what she knew now, she would have invested in a cab. Too late.

Lena Lane

The good news was that Jon had become an official family member. Apparently, the missing piece was coming to the rescue of the baby sister. As the official hero of the Sampson clan, he was welcome at any home, at any time, for any reason. Unfortunately, he had yet to take advantage of the offers. He had also been suspiciously absent from her presence.

Sharon knew he had been detained by the police for excessive force against The Suit. Not that she got this information from him directly. No. Peter Leveque, his old partner, had to tell her. Jon hadn't spoken to her since the incident.

She had called him, to thank him for coming to her rescue, but he hadn't answered. Wanting to do this in person, she'd left him a voicemail asking him to call her back. She was hoping to grab some dinner with him. When he didn't call the next day, she followed up with a text. Another day went by, and still no response. At that point, she texted a quick note, *Thanks for saving me.*

If he didn't want to see her again, that was fine. She could move on. Again.

Story Time

Sharon had had enough for one day and was getting ready to leave when the front door to the real estate office opened. *Son of a bitch.* She plastered her smile on her face and started thinking of a polite way to tell whomever just walked in to take a hike. But her words faded, along with her smile, when she saw Jon.

"'Ello, love." He stood by the door holding a bouquet of flowers and a box of chocolates. Her confusion must have been expressed on her face, because he presented them to her saying, "I hear this is what you get a woman when you've fucked up."

She snorted. "Is this your attempt at an apology?" Despite the question, she was happy to see him. At least he wasn't ghosting her again. Maybe she would be able to get some answers to the many questions she had for him before he disappeared permanently.

"Yes," he said simply.

Sharon took the bundle of twelve multicolored roses and the box from him, and with a nudge of her head, indicated that he should sit in the sitting area. She went to the back and got down a vase for the flowers. She took her time with them. Once they were in water, she opened the box of chocolates and leaned against the counter to enjoy a couple. Only when she estimated a full fifteen minutes had passed did she go back out.

"So, Mr. Rossi," she said while walking to where he sat, "what can I do for you?" She tried to ignore the sheepish grin on his face, or the deep, dark eyes that were laughing at her. He knew she'd kept him waiting on purpose. She had a feeling he didn't care.

"You can sit with me and listen to a story." He patted the cushion of the seat right next to his. "Please."

She would, happily. But she wasn't about to make it easy for him. "I hope it's quick. I've had a long day and was about to lock up when you came in."

He inclined his head in understanding. "I'll do my best."

Without another word, she sat across from him on the couch and crossed her legs. "Very well."

With a grin, he began, "Once upon a time, there was an evil man who forced himself on a young girl. Unfortunately, his evil seed planted. She wanted nothing to do with the child but still a minor, the girl wasn't able to get an abortion without her parents' permission. Also unfortunate, they were very religious and considered abortions very bad. Having heard that the girl was pregnant, the evil fucker decided he didn't want his child born a bastard, so he married her. The girl was forced to give birth to the child, but ashamed of what had happened, she ended her own life shortly after. The child was only a newborn babe at the time."

Well, this was not going where she thought it would.

"The evil father—and I use the term loosely—was a fucker who beat his child on a regular basis, especially when the magical potion of alcohol was involved. Anyway, when the child was nine, the authorities rescued, him and he went into foster care. Unlike most stories you've heard about the foster system, this kid was lucky and found a good mum to care for him. Oh, it wasn't perfect, of course. There were four other kids there by the time he arrived, and children in those types of situations are broken young, so it was rough for everyone. But she did her best with the four children in her care."

"Jon, honey…" Sharon interrupted gently, "What is this…?" Unfortunately, there were a lot of abused kids out there; the story was not uncommon. They were so morbid and depressing, all she wanted to do was cry and run away from them. Could this be *his* background? Why he never talked about himself?

He smiled sweetly and continued. "His foster mum never lied to him, so he grew up knowing who he was and where he came from. It was a dark background, and he vowed to make the darkness go away for other kids like him. He decided that when he was old enough, he would become an all-powerful policeman, and he'd use his powerful talisman—the almighty badge!—for the good of all girls and boys."

Oh my God, this was *his story.* Sharon didn't know what to think, how to feel. She couldn't imagine being a child of rape, abuse, and neglect. All of a sudden, she wanted to wrap her arms around him, hold him tightly until he forgot all about his parents. "Jon, there is no need for you to continue with this. Please stop…"

But the story didn't stop. "He did that for many years, and advanced to be a detective. But the darkness never got any better. Every time he defeated one bad buy, another would take his place. Over and over again. He became frustrated and angry. This wasn't working; he had to find another way.

"He decided that maybe, just maybe, he could teach women and children to defend themselves against the evil ones. He went to a faraway land, where he picked up a super sexy accent," at this point, Jon winked at her, "and learned all about the different types of defense moves and strategies. When he came back, he got derailed on his plan by a friendly side-quest, to see his best friend get married." He shrugged with a silly grin. "So he went on this journey to another land, this one not so far away, and met a gorgeous, platinum blond maiden with soulful blue eyes and ruby red lips he loved to kiss.

"Things were going very well with his lovely maiden, and he gave her quest of her own, which she was happy to help with," Jon paused and gave her a frown before continuing, "he *assumed*. But before that quest happened, he got some very bad news. His foster mum had passed away. He was forced to take another side-quest, a very painful one. He had to find her a final resting place. That took him far longer than he expected, and he never got a chance to apologize for being mean to the fair maiden."

Well, that explained why he had been such an asshole. The death of a loved one, even if not biologically related, hurt. Considering she sounded like a better human being than his biological parents, the pain must have been horrible. Her heart ached for him.

"Upon his return, the maiden was very angry with him and didn't want to talk to him. But then she was attacked by two dragons. And he lost his mind. Recalling everything that happened with his young mum, and what happened to others during his career as a detective, he became very angry, too. In his attempt to rescue the maiden, he beat the dragons up, really bad."

At this point in the story, she had to stifle her laugh. Yeah, he had beat them to a pulp. Sharon remembered his loss of control with The Suit and thought he might have killed him. She was really glad he didn't. For some reason, she didn't think outright murder would sit well with him.

VICTORIAN SURPRISE

"The dragons complained to local law enforcement, and he was taken to the local prison, where he was forced to explain himself for a full day.

"The poor maiden had no idea where he'd gone. All she knew was that he'd gone away. Wanting forgiveness, he went to the local magic makers and asked for something powerful that would make the beautiful maiden forgive him. They gave him two: a rainbow bouquet of illusion and a sugar potion. He's given both to the maiden, and now he waits for, hopefully, a happy ending.

"What do you think, Shae? Will the maiden forgive him for leaving her?"

Sharon sat there, stunned. This was the story of his life, his childhood, something he could have told her many times before, but he waited until now? "I'm sure the maiden understand how difficult his life has been. But that doesn't mean he's off the hook." She stood and went to join him on the couch, on the same cushion he had asked her to sit before. Needing the soothing comfort of a physical touch, she grabbed his hand from his lap and held it. "After I shared so much with you, after all the time we spent together, you couldn't have told me any of this sooner?"

"Sorry, love, but people don't like hanging out with a child of rape, son of a violent, drunken father and a mother who committed suicide. That is quite the recipe for mental illness." Shrugging nonchalantly, he said, "Trust me, I've learned from experience. I talk, and suddenly, something comes up. Then they scurry away, never to be heard from again." With a gentle touch, he tucked strands of her hair behind her ear. "This is the part where *you* run."

"Yeah?" She didn't think she would run, not because of this anyway. Granted, it was a lot of crazy information she wasn't expecting, and she would need time to process it, but she wasn't so afraid of him that she needed to bolt just yet. "I'm curious, how many have run?"

"All but Alyssa."

Ouch. That gave rejection *a whole new meaning.*

Sharon was afraid to ask, but she had to know. Hesitantly, she asked, "And your father?"

"Gone." His reply was cold with no hint of sadness. "Died in jail twelve years ago." The bitterness was clear as he finished, "And good riddance."

She couldn't imagine being abused by the one who should have given protection. Her father was far from perfect, but Jon's story was unfathomable.

Trying to lighten the mood a little bit, she hoped he'd catch the reference when she said, "Well, Adrian, it's time we head out." She waited long enough to know that he got the joke. As she watched the corner of his lip lift, she knew that he got it.

"Should I be insulted that you just referred to me as Satan's child?"

Walking to her office for her jacket and bag, she spoke over her shoulder. "Nah."

After that, they walked into the cold night together, in silence.

Too Perfect

Jon was cautiously optimistic while walking Shae to her car. If she could see past the mess that was his childhood, she'd be the first. Well, the first of his potential girlfriends. Aly didn't count because she was a mess herself, and they'd become friends out of necessity. But Shae was a normal person. She had been raised in a normal family, with siblings, aunts and uncles that cared about her, and friends who loved her unconditionally. Could she honestly not be concerned about the possibility of insanity taking over his mind?

That fear had been with him since he'd first learned that mental illness could be inherited. Not so much from his mother's side. Granted, her mental state may have been compromised by illness, but it didn't take much to believe all she wanted was peace.

She'd been so young, forced to marry the abusive fucktard that had assaulted her. He couldn't imagine how trapped she must have felt. It was also doubtful she knew anything about the options available to her. Though limited considering the norm at the time, there must have been something. If Jon could go back there, he would steal her away to a safe house somewhere. Protect her.

As for his sperm donor, he'd throw that bastard in jail as soon as he could. It's where he deserved to be. At least Jon no longer had to think about him.

When he had died, the department of corrections had asked Jon if he wanted to bury his father. Jon's response at the time had been less than cordial, "Burn that fucker up and flush his ashes down the toilet. That's all that piece of shit is good for." What they ended up doing with his body, Jon didn't know. Nor did he care. Since that call, he'd never looked back.

"Are you okay?" Shae asked, bringing him to the present.

They had arrived at her car and had been standing there for a bit, both lost in thought.

"Sure, love." There were too many things going through his mind, things he never wanted to think about again. But at least, he had no more secrets to hide.

"Listen, Jon," she began and he was immediately on edge. Those words were as good as, *We need to talk*. "We are both tired and we definitely need a good night sleep. So, let's go home and do that, okay?"

What? Did she just ask him to her place? After everything he'd just told her, he expected a good night and good riddance. "Excuse me?"

"Here's the thing. You're in emotional turmoil right now, having just bared your soul." She looked up at him and placed her hand on his chest. "So, I'm going to take you home with me. I'm going to offer you some milk and cookies. We're going to find a horrible B movie that you'll adore, then we'll fall asleep. And when the morning comes, we'll start the day fresh. How does that sound?"

She was going to make this easy on him; he couldn't believe it. "A little too perfect," he admitted.

When he decided to share the sordid details, he expected shock, fear, and not a little disgust. As he spoke his story, he saw those emotions, and more, flicker across her face. Shae may be a good actress, but not good enough to hide everything from him. What he hadn't seen was shame. Shame at having been with him. And it seemed she wasn't going to run.

What an incredible woman.

Night Sky

"I didn't see the skylight the last time I was here," Jon commented as he stared at the stars. He appeared comfortable with his arms crossed under his head.

Sharon was relaxed until he commented about the skylight. Lifting her head off his shoulder, she frowned at him. "What do you mean 'didn't see'? You've never been in my bedroom." When he didn't answer right away, she questioned, "Have you?"

"No, Shae," he responded with a chuckle, "I've never been in your bedroom." After a little head bobble, he corrected, "Until tonight, of course."

"Then what did you mean by that?" She wasn't going to let it go. "Because you've been known to cross the line, Jon."

Her tone must have told him she was serious, because he looked at her with a sad expression. "When I was here last, the bedroom door was open. That's all I meant."

"Oh." She felt stupid. Maybe she wasn't as open-minded as she thought. She settled down on his shoulder again and looked at the stars. Hoping to change the subject, she said, "That skylight is one of the reasons I bought this property. The view is incredible, especially on clear nights like this."

"It's amazing. I can see why you love it."

The silence stretched and the moment became awkward. Sharon didn't know how to make things better between them. Their relationship wasn't a deadline that could be addressed with an extension. It wasn't furniture in a living room that needed to be rearranged, or a leaky roof that could be patched. Their foundation had been rocked, and she had no clue what to do.

"Shae?" He broke the silence first.

"Hmm?"

"Can we have an honest conversation?"

No! Her mind screamed. That was just another way to say, *We need to talk,* and it was much too soon to discuss anything else that might send her world spinning. She still hadn't fully recovered from her assault and his nightmarish story. Instead, she took a fortifying breath and said, "Sure. What's up?"

"I know you believe things have changed drastically, considering what you now know. However," he turned slightly to look at her, "I am still the same person you spent time with in Vegas."

It was true. Just because she hadn't known his complete story at the time, it didn't change who he was as an individual. But there was still so much she didn't know about him. What if the rest was worse? What if he inherited his father's violent tendencies? Could she shrug those off? After all, what he did to the Suit was quite vicious. "I believe that, but you have to admit that I've only seen a piece of the person you are." Sharon began playing connect-the-dots with the freckles scattered across his chest and arms, acting like a carefree person, even though she was feeling far from it. "Tell me, Jonathan Rossi, who are you?"

His reply was slow coming. Just when she began to think he wouldn't respond at all, he said, "I don't know." She felt his shoulders lift in a shrug. "Who are any of us beyond our experiences, thoughts, and beliefs? Our actions."

Sharon chuckled. "Poet and philosopher, for sure." Her head rose when he shrugged again.

"I don't know about that, but I've seen a lot in my life, beginning with what I initially grew up with, which I believed was the norm. Once I realized it wasn't, once I saw how other people lived, I knew that I would do everything in my power to make sure no one else experienced what I had gone through."

"Yes, that's why you became a detective, but then you left. Why?" She paused, but then quickly clarified, "I know you said it was because there was always a new bad guy, but is that all?"

"Well..." Jon hesitated. "That world is very dark, Shae. You hear things in the news about gruesome or horrific scenes, and from there, you use your imagination. But unless you've been there, actually seen how gruesome, how horrific, those scenes truly are, you have no idea. You may think you do, but you don't.

"Beyond what you see, there are also smells which haunt you. They penetrate your clothes, seep into your hair, and even though you scrub everything in sight—especially yourself—something about the whole experience leaves you tainted.

"It's completely overwhelming, a nightmare; the sounds of screams, the smell of blood, the sight of pain and death. It can all leave you drained, and at night, you stare at the ceiling, unable to sleep, replaying everything over and over again in your mind."

Sharon thought she could understand, and his words left her incredibly sad. There might be pressure in the real estate world, but at least no one was screaming. Well, screaming in pain anyway. There was always the *princess* who thought she deserved hand holding service. Or there would be screaming.

"It got me thinking. I don't want to play catch up anymore. I don't want to be involved after those atrocities are committed, after the damage is done. I want those attacks to be *prevented*. And if I can't do that, then I can at least teach kids how to give the bastards a good fight."

She smiled and said, "Enter self-defense classes."

"You got it, love."

Closing Time

Shae had mentioned a few times that Jon had the heart of a poet. He didn't consider himself one. Maybe she was the reason? Because his world had never before included someone as loving, as understanding, and as passionate as the woman sitting beside him. Under the table, he reached for her hand and gave it a gentle squeeze. He'd have to thank her properly once they were home.

Since their nighttime talk, while staring at the stars, their relationship had returned to the easy companionship they had in Vegas, only better. Their lives had intermingled, and they spent more time together than apart. Even the stressful business of purchasing property didn't strain their bond.

They had gone to see various properties, but none held as much potential as the Victorian where Shae had been attacked. To his dismay, she had kept bringing it up. "I can't bring you back to the place you were attacked!" he'd argued. "That's just cruel."

"I will not be victimized, Jonathan," she'd insisted. "There's no better way to say 'fuck you' to those bastards than to go back and make that property our bitch." And when he'd tried to debate again, she challenged him, "Is it, or is it not, the best fit for your needs?" At that point, he'd had nothing else to say. She'd been right. So he had shrugged and let it go.

And in a few minutes, it would be officially his.

VICTORIAN SURPRISE

The closing attorney placed some papers in front of Jon for signature while explaining what they were. If he had known how many documents needed to be signed, he would have made a stamp before coming.
Eventually, though, there was an end. "Congratulations, Mr. Rossi," the attorney said as she stood. Extending her hand, she continued, "Please let me know when you're ready to start the classes. I'll be there."

"Thank you," Jon said, shaking her hand. "I'll be sure to do that." Finally. He had so many ideas; he was really looking forward to setting it all up and getting those classes started.

Once they were outside, Shae turned to him. "Happy?" she asked.

"Excited," he said. The way he saw it, this place was a new beginning for him. And he was thrilled that she was with him. "Shall we go see it?"

"Absolutely!" Shae seemed as eager about this as he was.

During the drive over, they discussed renovation plans, mostly for the first floor. Jon talked about what he needed to do to make it functional and safe. "The two upper floors I don't really care about. I just need a place to crash," he said nonchalantly. "I'll get to them when I get to them."

"No, no, no," Shae argued, just as her phone dinged. "As your girlfriend, I need a good, *clean* space to be with you." She started reading the text. "We can't always be hanging around my place." In a distracted voice, she concluded, "It's much too small."

Jon looked over at her for a quick second, stunned at her words, before returning his eyes to the road. "Um... Shae?"

She didn't bother to look up. Typing furiously on her cell, she barely acknowledged him, "Hmm?"

"I was just curious, love… when did we become an item?" Shouldn't this be something they discussed beforehand? He wasn't sure he knew all the rules regarding long-term relationships, considering his only attempt was with Aly back in high school. But they should really have a conversation about this. Not for his benefit, but for hers.

"Hmm?" Another quick glance over told him she was completely focused on her phone. Absently, she said, "Please give me a minute."

He shook his head.

This is what a relationship with her would be like, moments of incredible closeness and understanding, followed by being put on hold for undetermined lengths of time.

When she'd told him that she was constantly on the run, she wasn't kidding. There was always something. Even during Christmas and New Year's, there were still clients emailing and texting her. If she wanted a moment of peace, she had to turn it off. Which she did. After being asked, of course.

"Okay, honey," she finally put her phone down and looked at him. "What's up?"

Rethinking his question, Jon decided it was not the best time to discuss that topic. "Nothing, love. I was just agreeing with you."

Group Effort

The two of them were discussing ideal half-bath locations when Sammy walked in with Samantha. As soon as they were inside, Sharon screeched with glee and hurried over to hug them. She couldn't wait to share her surprise with Jon.

"I'm so glad you're here," she said stepping back. Turning to Jon, she said, "I have a present for you."

He was standing where she'd left him, with his hands in his pockets, his jacket pushed open to reveal his button-down shirt. Her memory flashed back to the first time she saw him, back at the airport. Things had certainly changed since then, but he looked as amazing as ever.

"Good to see you both," he said to the couple. "How are you enjoying married life?"

"You know," Samantha started, "it's not that different. I mean, we still live in the same house, so that hasn't changed. The only thing that's new is that we've started talking about getting a cat. Well, I want a cat. He wants a dog. But dogs are so much work, you know?" Barely pausing for breath, she continued, "You have to take them for walks, and I know there's plenty of property for him to run, but there are wild animals out there. And I'm a city girl, so I don't want to get lost in what is technically our backyard. Can you imagine? So I'm thinking a cat would be a better choice for us. She'd have plenty of space inside the house, and she'd be safe from wolves, you know?"

"Sam, honey," Sharon interrupted before Samantha took another breath and continued to talk their ears off, "I'm glad things are good with you and Sammy." Turning to her brother, she asked, "Did you bring it?"

Without a word, he handed her the long storage tube which had been hidden behind his back. She took it from him and hurried to the back room where there was a long bench against the back wall. "Come," she told the group. Once there, she opened the tube and pulled out the architectural designs she drew up.

She really hoped Jon would like them. As soon as his offer had been accepted, she began planning how to best reconfigure the living area upstairs and spent hours on the drawings. The dojo space was his baby; she'd leave that to him. The upstairs, though, he didn't really care much about. But she knew how important a living space was to a person—even if he didn't. That was going to be his home; it wasn't just shelter, it would become a haven. A place of his own that he'd never had. She knew he'd come close with his rentals. But *owning* a space was a whole different experience.

After unrolling the designs and laying them flat, Sharon turned to Jon smiling and said, "Surprise."

His dark brows drew together in a frown as he stepped closer to see. She knew he couldn't really read them, but she would be happy to help him. His voice was soft when he asked, "Did you draw these?" She nodded. "For me?" She nodded again. The frown faded, and was quickly replaced with a grin. "Show me," he said, right before looking at the papers again.

Her worry that he might not appreciate her work diminished with his enthusiasm. He poured over the plans, tracing the lines with his finger, wanting to see what she envisioned for him. She was so happy at that moment, she thought her heart would explode.

"Sam, honey, can I please have the tablet?" Shockingly, Samantha handed it to her without saying anything. Probably because Sammy was holding her hand, squeezing it tightly, a tactile request to keep her quiet. "Jon, look."

The video she played was a walk-through of what the property would look like when finished. Not only did it include the floor plan she designed, but it was also furnished as she imagined. Bright, open spaces with clean lines and warm colors. Big comfy furniture that he could relax in. And in the bedroom, a skylight right above the king-sized bed.

"This is brilliant!" She could hear the excitement in his voice; it mirrored her own.

It sounded like he loved the design as much as she did, but she wanted to make sure he knew the final decisions were his. "It's just a plan. We're happy to make whatever changes you'd like."

That caught his attention, and he looked up. "We?"

"I drew the design, but Sammy will make it happen." She raised her hand to indicate her brother who was standing quietly by the window. "And Sam here," she indicated Samantha who was checking her phone, "will help by picking the best products to use." She looked up and gave him a sweet smile.

Sharon could tell by his expression that he was shocked. Considering what had happened between Jon and Sammy in Vegas, she couldn't blame him. They hadn't had the best of introductions.

"Group effort, eh?" His gaze bounced from one person to another, but the only one who was watching him was Sharon. Sammy was still looking out the window, and Samantha was still looking at her phone.

Without turning, Sammy said, "The project can be completed before spring."

A second wave of surprise for him. "Wow, that's pretty quick."

"Anything for my baby sis." Sammy finally turned and walked over to Jon. "And the man who saved her." In an unusual move, he stuck his hand out. When Jon took it, he said, "Thanks."

At some point, Sharon would have to tell Jon just how extraordinary that was. He had no idea what kind of person her antisocial brother was.

After the handshake, both Sams headed out, leaving Sharon and Jon alone.

"I can't believe you did this," Jon said, looking at the tablet again, his voice full of awe.

"Oh honey," she joked, "don't make too much of a big deal about it. Remember, it's what I enjoy doing. It was nothing." Inside, though, she was thrilled that he loved it as much as she did. She wouldn't say it, but she could see herself living here, once it was all redone, of course.

Hearing the lie for what it was, he turned and hugged her. "Sure, love, whatever you say." He kissed her on her forehead, but then lifted her chin to look into her eyes. "I will never forget this," he vowed.

"Oh, I know," she said in a heated vixen voice. Gripping his lapels and pulling him down, she whispered against his lips, "I won't let you." She kissed him then, deeply.

Such Wickedness

What had been intended to be a sweet exchange became intensely passionate, fueled by emotions neither of them were ready to share.

Goosebumps erupted over her body as she reached up to lock her arms around his nape, pulling him closer, keeping him there. Their lips met and parted, each kiss becoming more urgent than the one before.

He answered by wrapping his arms around her waist, and holding her body tightly against his. She opened her mouth to him, an invitation, and sighed when his tongue swept through it quickly. It left her wanting more, much more. *That was such a Jon move.* Out of breath, she pulled back, but just long enough to confirm he was as hungry for her as she was for him. When she saw the hunger in his eyes, heard his heavy breathing, felt his fists gripping her suit at her hips, she knew. He was as gone as she.

"Such wickedness," Sharon said with a grin, right before she nibbled his lips. Immediately, she kissed them better.

His hands came up to frame her face as his lips devoured her mouth. Over and over again, they kissed, their lips and tongues coming together, breaking apart only to breathe.

As he moved his kisses to her jaw and neck, he slid a hand down her back, the move somehow bringing them closer together; something she didn't think was possible. She leaned back to give him better access.

Sharon shut her eyes tightly, acutely aware of her belly spinning wildly, her nipples hardening, the tingle between her legs begging for his touch. Moaning, she arched her back and cried out with pleasure when he grabbed a breast, hard.

Jon's voice was hushed and heavy, his dark eyes hooded with desire, when he asked, "That's enough, no?"

She knew what he was asking. "Yes," she confirmed quickly, "it's enough foreplay!" Skillfully, she undid the button of his pants, slipping her hand in to feel the hard length of him. The zipper slid and the pants dropped to his knees.

While she stroked him, he went through his wallet for a condom and soon as it was in place, he bundled her suit skirt out of the way, and lifted her onto the bench. He tugged her panties off and carelessly threw them to the floor behind him. Soon after, he was positioning her legs over his forearms and he slammed into her.

"Yes!" Sharon screamed at being so full. She held onto his shoulders, afraid she'd fall. Each thrust sent incredible sensations through her, the pressure building so quickly, she thought she would burst. Her moans became cries. The cries became screams of pleasure. Tighter and tighter, the tension grew, until she was exploding, her body trembling as waves of ecstasy washed over her.

It wasn't long before she felt him shudder as he climaxed, his growl of satisfaction making her shiver.

Sated, he leaned into her and laid his head against her shoulder while still supporting both of them by gripping the bench. Her arms wrapped around him, and she drew lazy circles on his back with her nails.

VICTORIAN SURPRISE

"God, I love that," Sharon whispered into his neck, still a little breathless.

"What?" More of a mumbled sound than a spoken word.

"The primitive sound you make when you finish," she clarified.

He lifted up just far enough to look at her. "That's good, Shae." There was an intensity in his penetrating gaze that she hadn't seen before. Somehow, his dark eyes seemed darker. The void called to her, begged her to stay. "I love that about you, too. How you cry out. How you hold me tight." His laugh was humorless. "How you make me feel like you don't want to let go."

The conversation had taken an unexpected turn. Sharon didn't know what happened, but things had become far more intense than just *breaking the new place in*. "Yeah?" She reached out for the curl that kept landing on his forehead and spun it around her finger. She tugged it lightly and said, "Maybe that's because I don't want to," she paused for a heartbeat, "let you go." A strange magic had woven around them, and she had the impression that a thousand words had been shared with just those few.

Jon gave her a gentle smile while he caressed her cheek with the back of his hand. But then he pulled away from her. "I should…" He looked down and took care of the condom.

The moment had passed.

Back to normal, she said, "Good idea." She jumped off the counter and tugged her skirt down. "I don't know about you, but I'm thinking lunch would be awesome. What do you think?"

"I think you're brilliant."

The Talk

Jon left the bathroom after his shower with nothing but his boxers on. As he walked toward the kitchen, he was struck by the homey scene he was a part of and froze. Sharon was pouring some coffee into two mugs at the counter. The table was already set for two: a couple of plates, a couple of forks. In the center of it was a plate of bacon, and he could see bagels in the toaster oven.

When had this happened? Why hadn't he noticed sooner? Were they a *couple?*

She never officially asked him to move in. Hell, they'd never even had the *girlfriend-boyfriend* talk. Not that he had anyone else in his life. Nor would he. Sharon was *it*. The one and only for him. But these are things that people should know about themselves, no? Since their talk about his background a couple of months ago, when he'd told her all of his dark secrets, she'd invited him back every night. He spent more time there than at his own place.

In a daze, he took his usual seat at the table and looked around at the familiar space.

"Good morning, honey," Sharon placed his usual mug in front of him while bending over to kiss him on the cheek. "How did you sleep?" She walked around and sat to his left. Her usual spot.

"Sharon, we need to talk." The moment the words were out of his mouth, he could have kicked himself. *Damn it! You never, ever, say those words.*

VICTORIAN SURPRISE

The cup she held never made it to her lips. It stopped midway as she waited for *The Talk*.

"No, I don't mean it like that," he retracted swiftly. He reached out and gently touched her forearm. He would have taken her hand, but it was holding a hot cup of coffee, one that she might aim at his head if he didn't make things clear. And quickly.

She didn't reply; she simply took a sip of her coffee and waited. Her sharp gaze followed his every move.

"Sorry, love." After gulping coffee from his mug, he said, "What I meant was, I need clarification." Putting it down, he gazed at her face, taking note of her porcelain skin, her crystal eyes, her natural lips. He would commit her face to memory now, just in case. He took a deep breath, and with his detective skills on high alert, he asked, "Why am I here?"

At first, she frowned in confusion. Jon noted her slight head shake, observed her micro shrug. He watched her watch *him* as she processed the question. Glad that she didn't given him a dismissive answer, he patiently waited as she sorted out her thoughts. At last, she answered simply and honestly, "Because I love you." Without breaking eye contact, she grabbed a piece of bacon. "And I don't want you to go anywhere."

His stomach spun, then dropped. *Did she? Could she?!* After so many years of believing he would die alone, he couldn't believe it. "Are you sure?" He swallowed nervously. "Because I can't change who I am."

"Well, that's good, considering I wouldn't want you to change." Nonchalantly, she drank her coffee.

"I can't have kids," he pushed. Did she truly understand what she was saying? Did she know that he came with the baggage of his childhood?

"Well, that's good," her frown returned, "because I don't want any." After a short pause, she asked, "I'm curious, why not?"

"Because mental illness is sometimes inherited. And I wouldn't want any child of mine going nuts because of me." Jon could think of nothing more terrifying than being responsible for breaking an innocent child before birth.

"Oh, honey," Shae put her mug down and gently covered his hand with hers. "You are not nuts; far from it. You are sweet, and kind, and everything a woman would want as the father of her children." But then she shrugged. "If she wanted children. All I want are nieces and nephews to spoil." Taking her hand back, she challenged him. "It's your turn. Why are you here?"

Without hesitation, he echoed her words. "Because I love you." He caressed her cheek and tucked a couple of wispies behind her ear. "And I don't want to go anywhere."

Welcome Home

"Faster!" Jon yelled at her.

Jab, cross, hook, uppercut. Jab, cross, hook, uppercut. In smooth succession, Shae punched the pads he held. *Jab, cross, hook, uppercut.* Sometimes, she watched herself in the big floor-to-ceiling mirror of the dojo floor, amazed at the progress she'd made in the past few months. All thanks to him.

"Roundhouse!" he pushed.

But if he kept pushing her, she was going to practice her self-defense forms on *him*. "For the love of all that is holy, have mercy!" Instead of kicking the pad as he demanded, she dropped to the mat, landing flat on her back, gasping for breath. "I need a break or I'm going to pass out."

He stood over her and nudged her side with a foot. "Come now, only five more minutes, and you can stretch."

"Five minutes?! You said 'five minutes' five minutes ago." She slapped the mat for emphasis. "You are a cruel taskmaster, Jonathan Rossi."

"And you're going to be late to your showing if you don't move your delectable ass." He tried to nudge her again, but she grabbed his ankle and pulled it from under him. With her other hand, she pushed the other foot out. Losing his balance, he fell to the mat, landing with a thud. With the air knocked out of him, he sounded breathless when he said, "That was a good move, love."

"I learned from the best." She rolled over on her side and got up with a grunt. "But no more. For today. I'm going upstairs to shower." But as she took her first step, pain radiated from her butt cheek. Immediately, she slapped a hand on it. "Ooh, ooh, ooh, why does my ass hurt?!"

"Pain is weakness leaving the body," was his uncaring reply. He stood and began walking to the backroom.

It was a line she'd heard from him every time she complained her body ached from the classes he'd given her over the past few months. But this one was different. "No, Jon, I'm serious." The ache went up to her lower back and down to her upper thigh. She rubbed it, trying to make it better, but it didn't help. "I think you broke my ass. What did you do?"

When he returned to her, she saw him trying to hide his amused grin. "This happens occasionally, because of the muscle tightening. It needs to relax so that the blood flow can recover." He wrapped an arm around her and began to squeeze her butt cheek. "Massaging the area a few times—every day—will help." It wasn't long before her other butt cheek was getting similar attention. He grinned.

"Aw, honey," Shae put her hands on his shoulders and gave him an exaggerated smile. "You're so sweet, helping me like this, massaging me where I need it most." Though she didn't want to admit it, his hands were helping. The ache was fading fast. As much as she was enjoying his touch, she did have things to do. "Alright, alright, it's all better now. I have to go." She walked over to the back room, and stopped at the bottom of the stairs. "Oh my God, Jon…" Pulling

VICTORIAN SURPRISE

herself up the first step, she complained, "So many steps." She pulled herself up to the second one.

Before she stepped on the third, he came from behind her and placed his hands on her butt again, this time pushing her up. "Do you think your brother could add an elevator?"

"I don't see why not..." She would definitely talk to Sammy about that, because their bedroom was on the third floor, and there were a lot of stairs. Far too many. "Whose idea was it to get this place, anyway?"

"I do believe it was yours, love," he said, still pushing her up.

"Okay, next time, don't listen to me."

But she didn't think there would be a next time. When they finally reached the top floor, she looked at their home and fell in love with it again. It was made for them, just them.

Standing in the center of the room, she looked at everything. All around them were touches of their life together. Pictures of them dancing at Aly and Emily's wedding. Pictures of the renovation and the fun they'd had breaking everything down. Pictures of family gatherings, where her bunch embraced him, made him one of their own. Pictures of her family, which included Aly and Emily, especially after her cancer went into remission. In each one, they were together. And happy.

Jon.

He was the missing piece her heart had always needed.

Reading her thoughts, he wrapped his arms around her from behind and, for the millionth time, whispered, "Welcome home, love."

Colonial Offer
Book One of the Sampson Series

Sarah was content—or so she'd thought. Numbly going through each day believing she didn't need anything more, she hadn't been looking for love. Not until she met a real estate agent that sent her belly spinning with unexpected thrills. What will she do with the man who sent her life into a roller-coaster ride she couldn't control?

Scott was busy. The family business was running him ragged and he had barely enough time to keep his sanity. But some distractions cannot be ignored, and Sarah was too tasty a morsel to overlook—each nibble just made him want more. Could he convince her that he could give her what she never thought she'd needed?

In their real estate world where bids are often rejected, will she accept his final offer?

VICTORIAN SURPRISE

Cabin Rescue
Book Two of the Sampson Series

Samuel is focused on his business and doesn't like complications, especially when they come from a tenacious woman who loves to push his buttons—all of them. With long legs and kissable lips, she's a distraction he doesn't need. So when she persuades him to hire her for his company, is he making the biggest mistake of his life?

Samantha knew she wanted to be a part of Suziq Construction from the moment she saw its website—and its owner. The successful business was ideal for her, as was the sexy brute who owned it. Now, she just has to convince the owner that she's perfect for the company—and for him.

And when her world turns upside down and she's left homeless, will he come to her rescue?

Made in the USA
Middletown, DE
27 May 2018